A Thin Line Between

Regret & Redemption

A Novella written by D. D. Miles

Dedications

This book is dedicated to all of the creative geniuses that have inspired me. Heaven only knows what you mean and meant to me. I salute you.

Acknowledgments

First giving all honor and glory to God, I'd like to thank my mother, Janice Williams for her loving support. It's not every day that you have an avid reader, who so happens to be a retired Language Arts teacher, at your disposal. So if my subjects and verbs do not agree, or perhaps you come across some misspelled words, blame her. I'm just kidding, but thank you, mommy, for everything. You are priceless. To my dad, Larry Gosha who is my cheerleader and so supportive. I thank you, dad, for everything as well; your encouragement matters greatly. Thank you to my family and friends for your support as well. As you can see, I can't take full credit for any of this. I am so grateful to those who have come into my life to inspire and motivate me. To you, I say thank you as well.

To the Reader: I thank you for taking out the time to read this novella series. You're just one page away from an explosive romantic drama. Let's Go!

Chapter 1

BENJAMIN

Christmas Day...

"What's this?" I asked her.

"Open it. I'm dying to know what it says myself. It took all I had not to open this envelope before you did." She said. I read the letter.

Dear Terrance Robinson,

This letter will answer any and all questions of paternity. As it regards Cameron B. Harris, subject A and Terrance Robinson, subject B. As a result, ninety-nine point ninety percent out of one hundred percent proves that you, Terrance Robinson, can be excluded as the biological father of Cameron B. Harris.

Once I read the word excluded, I dropped to my knees and closed my eyes. It was over for my marriage. I just knew it, and I didn't know what else I could say or do to get it back. It wasn't as strong as it once was, and what I feared the most just happened. I didn't know how Tamara would take this news, and it hurt the hell out of me to think she might leave me because of it.

Tamara called my name, snapping me out of my thoughts.

"Ben."

I opened my eyes and gazed up at her. I almost lost it. At that very moment, I wanted to release what many would consider a sign of weakness.

"What does it say?" She asked softly.

She probably already knew from my reaction. I tried to respond the best I could. "It said that. It said that, um." I couldn't find the words. "Um, I'm sorry, but whomever this dude, Terrance Robinson, is, was not the father of Cameron. Babe, where did you get this letter from?" I asked her.

"Say what!" she said, snatching the letter from my hands to read it for herself.

"Babe, I know this isn't what we planned, but-" was all I could say before she left the room.

I had so many emotions to hit me at once, but more importantly, the reality of losing my wife is what mattered to me the most. I went to look for Tamara. We really needed to talk about what that letter meant and what we were going to do about it.

I found her sitting down on our bed, staring at the letter. I knew this was like pouring salt into an open wound. But somehow, I hoped there would be some sign from her indicating that she was ready to talk about it.

Tamara sat in silence as I sat next to her.

"I, um, I just wanted to tell you how sorry I am for all of this," I said, reaching for her hand. "I know this isn't easy for you, and I thank you for sticking by me. Babe, for the rest of my life, I will never forgive myself for hurting you like this. I know I can't undo the past, and if I had the opportunity to do it all over again, I would. Nothing is worth destroying the love we share. I know this road isn't an easy one, and you have done more than enough, but I really need you by my side. Your having my back, babe, means everything to me. You just don't know how tough these past weeks have been for me. Stacey had given me the runaround about getting a paternity test, saying we needed to wait until Cameron was six weeks old. I should've known something was up when she insisted on me signing the birth certificate without any proof of paternity."

"Did you sign the birth certificate?" She asked.

"**HELL NAH!** I wasn't about to sign anything, especially not before knowing if he was mine or not. That's when she basically kicked me out of her hospital room because I wouldn't."

"So what about now? Are you going to sign it? He has your last name and everything."

"Give me some credit, Tamara. I'm not stupid. This is far from being over."

"Humph."

"What does that mean?" I asked.

"Nothing. Where are my Christmas gifts?" she asked, changing the subject as if she wasn't interested in answering my question.

I was bothered about how she responded to my not being stupid. As hard as it was, I decided not to get into it with her about it. Usually, I am good at reading people, but she wasn't giving me anything to go off of. Tamara had shut down on me emotionally. Months ago, she was so livid about Stacey, the baby, everything. Now, nothing. I knew what my next move was going to be, but I wanted her on board when I made it.

This was Christmas Day, and despite what I'd read or how I felt, I wasn't about to ruin this Christmas for anyone. So I pulled my bride into my arms to hold her as tight as I possibly could, and in my deepest, sexist voice, whispered, "I'm it." I told her.

"No, really, where is it?" She said, pulling out of my arms.

"Girl, I know you didn't just. Are you trying to say I'm not good enough for you?" I asked, feeling slightly rejected.

"Nope, but I know that you'd better come better than that."

"Oh, okay. Whateva, man. You really know how to mess up a moment, you know that?"

"You got all day for that. I love Christmas just as much as you do, remember? So, gimmie my gifts."

"Just close your eyes," I sighed. "You've already ruined the mood. Now, hold your hand out."

She did as instructed. I placed a black box in her hand with a gold bow on it. "Now open your eyes."

She opened the box quickly.

"Okay, it's a keyless remote to your car. Did you hide my presents in your car?" she asked excitedly.

I sighed. "Follow me."

I took her by the hand, and led her through the living room into the kitchen, and opened the door that led to the garage.

"Press start," I told her.

While she was doing that, I pressed the button on the wall to open the garage door.

"OH MY GOD! No, you didn't!" She said, covering her mouth.

Her face was lit up like our Christmas tree. This is the joy I always wanted to keep on my wife's face.

"Babe, do you like it?" I asked, wrapping my arm around her waist once she stopped jumping up and down.

"OH MY GOD! How did you know? I mean, hold on. Is this mine?" She said, asking about her 2025 Maserati GT.

"Yes, sweetheart, it's yours." I had to laugh at her. Tamara was acting as if she'd won her dream car on The Price Is Right. "So I take it that you like it then?"

"Yes! I love this car. I even test-drove it in Dallas."

"I know. That was the purpose. At least you got the car you wanted. I still have to wait on mine, but I am not tripping, though. Once Phillip told me how much you loved it, I knew I had to buy it for you.”

“I love it so much, babe. Thank you.”

“You’re very welcome, sweetheart, but it’s cold as hell out here. Can we go inside now? I even fixed us breakfast.” I told her.

We walked back into the house and sat down at the table to eat our breakfast. I made us bacon omelets with lots of cheese, just the way we love them, along with a stack of pancakes.

After helping Tamara clear the dishes off the table, I leaned over and kissed her on the cheek. She looked so happy while standing there at the sink. I knew we only had a few hours left together before going over to my parent’s house, and I just wanted to tell her how truly happy she had made me. Despite the latest news, we had a very bright future ahead of us.

“Have I told you how much I love you lately?” I asked, leaning against the counter.

“Yes, you have, but I never get tired of hearing it.” She

sweetly replied.

"Can I talk to you for a moment?"

"Sure." She rinsed the dish suds off her hands and dried them off.

She met me in the living room, where I sat her down on my lap.

"First, I want to thank you once again for my gifts. You will never know how much they meant to me. I don't know how or where you got that letter from, but I'm so glad you did. I felt like I was going to lose you, and I'm sorry for everything I put us through. I never meant to bring strife and confusion into our marriage. My only goal in life is to be the best husband to you and a great father to our children. Girl, you are my life, and I just want you to know that you are everything to me. I can't imagine living life without you. Thank-you. Thank-you. Thank-you." I said kissing, her with each gratitude. I couldn't have loved her more at that moment.

The next thing I knew, we had found ourselves naked and

spreading Christmas cheer from the living room to the bedroom.

We found what we needed the most in each other. In body, soul,

and spirit, we found togetherness.

Chapter 2

TAMARA

I know Ben thought I was acting cold to him, but I was just numb. I didn't have anything left for him and this baby situation anymore. Now, knowing this thing with Stacey was far from being over, it was time to find out if Ben was the father of her child, for sure. She had two men on the hook for one baby.

One phone call was all it took to get into contact with Terrance. I was hoping to free my husband from Stacey's web of lies, but at least Terrance is free. I went a step further to explain to his wife, Elise, how manipulative Stacey really was and all she'd done. Elise and Terrance shocked Stacey when they came together to demand a paternity test before she and the baby left the hospital. I purposely kept Ben's copy of the letter sealed in hopes of a different result, but I knew. When I spoke to Terrance to get a copy of his results a week ago, all he could say was, I can't believe it. So, I talked to Elise, and she shared the results with me.

I needed my husband to understand the strain this has placed on our marriage but it was not in jeopardy. I allowed him to speak his peace, but I have yet to speak mine. How things would end between them regarding paternity would be anyone's guess. She was trying to play the long game, but I had the cheat codes.

We were on our way to his parent's house for Christmas dinner. I had a big surprise for Ben. His nosey butt was going to be blown away. I caught him snooping around the house and Christmas tree a few times, looking to see what I had gotten him.

I was holding my cell phone, hoping it would ring soon. We were less than five minutes away from his folk's house. I couldn't wait to see Ben's face. If he thought that letter and the other gifts were something, then he was going to pass out behind this one. My phone rang, and I knew exactly who it was.

"Hey," I answered, trying hard to mask my excitement. I turned the radio up a little in hopes of it drowning out my caller's voice.

"Hey, you. Merry Christmas!" He said.

"Merry Christmas to you, too."

"I'm guessing by your tone, he's right next to you?"

"Un-huh."

"Well, I won't keep you, but I'm about five minutes away. Are you guys there, or close?"

"Uh, almost."

"All I need is a yes or no. We don't want to give too much away." Phillip said.

"Yes," I said with a girlish giggle. We had just pulled up in front of his parent's house.

"I will see y'all in a minute. Bye."

I didn't say anything else. I pressed end call on my phone and turned the radio back down.

"If I didn't know any better, I would've thought you were on the phone with a man," Ben said.

I cleared my throat. "How do you know that I wasn't?" I asked in a sassy but sexy tone.

"How do I know you weren't? Okay, settle my curiosity. Who was the man on the phone that is about to catch these hands for calling my wife?" He asked sternly.

"What if I said it was Pop?" I asked, still teasing.

"But that wasn't Pop. So who was it?"

I can't believe he was serious. "If you say so," I said with a smirk.

He got out, slamming the driver's side door of my brand new car. As he walked around to open my door, he looked like he had swallowed ten lemons.

"So, are you admitting to talking to another man? Disrespecting me, our marriage, and my love for you?"

He was being so stupid about nothing. "The answer is yes, but I was not being disrespectful."

"How in the hell do you figure you're not being disrespectful by talking to some other man on the phone in my presence? How could you do this and on Christmas Day at that? **WHO WAS THAT ON THE PHONE, TAMARA?!**" He yelled.

I would've laughed in his face if I didn't know that he was serious, but to do that now would only add fuel to his raging fire. So I did what any normal person in my position would do, looked at his stupid butt as if he were crazy.

"I ASKED YOU A QUESTION! Maybe you didn't understand me the first time, so let me ask you again slowly, **WHO-THE-HELL-WERE-YOU-TALKING-TO-ON-THE-PHONE?!"** He shouted each word in my face. I'd never seen him act like this, especially towards me.

Now, he was just doing too much, yelling at me as if I were some child.

"I was on the phone with Phillip. **ARE-YOU-HAPPY-NOW?!"** I yelled back.

The look of shock and disgust was on his face. But before Ben could say anything else, Phillip came driving down the street in Ben's car, blowing the horn and wearing a gigantic smile. By now, everyone in his parent's house had just about come outside to see his reaction.

When he saw his Corvette ZR1, his frown had turned upside down in mere seconds, and I suppose in that moment he forgave everything, but I hadn't. I only had these remaining words for him. **"Merry Christmas, dumbass,"** I told him and walked away, grabbing Erica by the arm, pulling her into the house and up to Ben's old bedroom, closing the door behind us.

"Girl, what's up?" Erica said, looking concerned.

"Ben has ruined Christmas for me," I said, rolling my eyes.

"How?"

"I gave him his first gift, which was the paternity results."

"I take it was good news if both of you are here together."

"No, but at the moment, I will be the first to tell you that I am unsure where this leaves us. I have to give it up to Terrance and his wife. They helped me out big time. I had gone to his office right after I got back from Dallas. I basically explained to him that Stacey told my husband that he might be the father of her child. He didn't like that one bit because, apparently, she had been telling him the same. The next day, he called and told me he had a paternity test done. He promised to make me a copy of the results. I asked him if he could keep my copy sealed because I wanted Ben to be the one to read it first. He understood and helped me, and I did him a solid by talking to Elise. I'm not saying that they will get back together or anything, but she has a better understanding of how Stacey manipulates people. "

"That's good, because I wasn't sure what would happen between those two."

"Kind of what's going on right now between Ben and me. You should have seen him, Erica. He had acted a plum fool outside. Earlier today, we had a heart-to-heart and were in a good space, but he had to ruin everything by wanting to know who I was on the phone with. I just wanted to surprise his stupid butt with his main gift, but no, that wasn't good enough for him. He couldn't leave well enough alone."

"Maybe Tamara, he's afraid that you will pay him back for what he has done to you."

"But he doesn't know if I would or wouldn't. All he's doing is looking out for himself. How he spoke to me just now was nasty."

I was not trying to hear that crap or to be the least bit sympathetic towards him.

"Well, check out my situation. TJ spent Christmas Eve with JJ at Jasmine's house last night. According to him, he went over there to put JJ's toys together but ended up falling asleep on her sofa. So naturally, I went off because he hadn't told me anything. He claimed he told me he was going over there a week ago. I know I have pregnancy brain at times, but come on. All I know is when I woke up this morning, he wasn't there."

"So, what are you saying? Do you think he is fooling around with Jasmine?"

"All I'm saying is I know my man's appetite, and he's

not getting fed here. So somebody is serving him up because the boy is on a three-meals-a-day diet, and I've been acting like a third-world country as of late. Everything he does aggravates me." Erica said.

"I'm with you when you're right. When they start acting up, shut down the kitchen until they get their act together. Lots of cold showers and a bad case of blue balls should bring them around." We had to high-fived each other on that one. "But girl, what about us? We may suffer, too." I told her after thinking about it.

"Uh-un, that's what they make small hand-held devices and batteries for."

"Girl, please, you remember what that song said about B.O.B back in the day, aka the battery-operated boyfriend?" We both laughed because we knew it was so true. "B.O.B don't lie or cheat and is home every night."

"And is." She agreed.

"Period."

Chapter 3

BENJAMIN

I know I've messed up. No one had to tell me. I knew it.

"Son, how do you like your uh, what do you kids called them, uh whips? That's it. How do you like your new whip?" My dad asked.

"I love it, Pop. Tamara got me good with this one, though."

"How's that?"

"She told me they had sold the car, and they wouldn't have another one until or after Christmas."

Laughing, he said, "Yeah, I know. It had been here in the garage for two weeks. It's sporty! I felt tempted to drive it myself."

"So you were in on it, too?"

"Yeah, we all were. That's why we all came outside when Phillip pulled it around the corner. We wanted to see the expression on your face, son." He said, slapping his hand on my shoulder.

"So she likes to hide my presents at your house. That's good to know, Pop."

"Now, wait a minute. Don't go telling Tamara I told you that."

"Uh-uh, too late, you told me already."

"Where is she, anyway?" Dad said, looking around.

"She's in the house."

"Oh."

"Yeah, I'm in the doghouse. Basically, before y'all came out. I was about to show my entire a- uh, I mean, my butt."

"Well, get your a-, I mean your butt in the house and make-up. Tamara is a good woman, Ben. Don't mess up your good thing. You hear me, son?"

"Yes, sir."

"Alright now."

After I spoke to everyone and kissed Ma on the cheek, I looked around the house for my wife.

"Hey TJ, have you seen Tamara and Erica?"

"Nah, dawg, but if they ain't down here, there's only one other place they could be."

"Upstairs bedroom." We said in unison.

I gave him a pound and made my way upstairs.

I stood outside the door and heard them laughing and giggling. So, I automatically knew it was about me. Not to be rude or to intrude, I knocked on my old bedroom door.

"Who is it?" Tamara asked with an attitude.

"It's me. Can we talk?"

"No." I knew that wasn't anybody, but Erica's smart mouth.

Then she opened the door. So I spoke.

"Erica."

"Benjamin." She replied, being very formal.

"What's up with that? Are you mad at me, too?" I asked her as she waddled past me.

"Un-huh, I'll see you downstairs, girl. Don't take too

long." She told Tamara.

"Don't worry, Erica, I won't." She said, rolling her eyes at me. "I'll be down in a minute."

I came into the room and closed the door behind me. Tamara turned her back to me. I stepped up behind her, wrapped my arms around her waist, and kissed her on the back of the neck.

"I know I'm beginning to sound like a broken record, but babe, I am really sorry." I said, softly.

"Seems like that's all you can be lately. Especially nowadays." She said, turning around and facing me.

"Tamara, that's not fair. Look, it has been a crazy couple of months. Our wedding was almost called off, and now it is a very good possibility that I am a father. I know it's frustrating and I'm sorry, but I can't help but wonder when the other shoe is going to drop."

"So are you saying because you were off having an affair when we first met, that I'm supposed to pay you back the same way? Gee, thanks, Ben. I must get started on that right away."

"You know what, Tamara? You might play the innocent role, but I'm not alone in this."

"What do you mean you aren't alone?!" she said, yelling.

"First, lower your voice in my parent's house, and second, be careful of who you let kiss you in elevators."

The look on her face was priceless. She really thought I didn't know, but I had known about it for a while. I just didn't trip about it. When I proposed to Tamara, I knew she was about to tell me, but I stopped her.

"Yeah, that's right. I knew about your ex, Marcus, kissing you. I saw it all. You forgot that I own the building, baby. I hardly miss anything."

Chapter 4

TAMARA

He had me by knowing about the kiss with Marcus, but I
hid my inner smirk. He knew it all and nothing at the same time.
He was acting so arrogantly. He didn't know about the close
calls between Phillip and me, but then again, if he had known, I
wouldn't have been here.

"And just in case you're wondering, we don't have
cameras in our offices or bathrooms, of course, but cameras are
everywhere else."

"Thanks for letting me know, but in my defense, I tried to
tell you, but you wouldn't let me." I said.

"I know I didn't. It was because of what I had done that I
wanted a new start for us. It may take us going to counseling, but
I want our marriage to work. I can promise you this," he said,
grabbing my hands. "I will never allow anything like this to ever
happen to us again. And if you find me acting a little tense
around you being around other men, just know, it's something I

got to work through. Honestly, my jealousy kicked into overdrive when we were at the Christmas party." He confessed. "If TJ hadn't stopped me, I would have ruined my reputation, business relationships, and friendship. Phillip had me tight last night. He knows what's up, and although we hadn't discussed things yet, our business partnership could have been on the line. I've never been the jealous type, babe, but seeing the two of you together like that, sent something through me, man. I just had a bad feeling, and it was about to be on from there, and you saw how upset Kherington was, and they aren't even together anymore. I know she thought the same thing that I had that it was very inappropriate. I heard she walked out on him after we left."

"She can't be too upset. She's with him today." I said, now smirking.

"That's because I invited her. They didn't come together. And just so we are clear. You are to never dance the way you did with another man as long as you are married to me. Don't let this handsome face fool you." He warned as he grabbed and pulled me closer to him. "Have I made myself clear?"

"As crystal. Can you let me go now?" I asked.

"Nope."

"Why not?"

"Because you hadn't kissed me yet."

"And I don't plan to."

"Really, but you will."

"No, I wo-"

He kissed me with so much passion that I almost forgot where we were. Remembering, I broke our embrace, before he successfully had my sweater over my head like he was attempting to do.

"We can't do this in your parent's house."

"Come on, Tamara, I need you to help me release this pent-up frustration."

"Uh-uh, we are not about to make love in your parent's house."

"Who said anything about making love? I promise it'll be

real quick." He said, kissing me on my neck and working his was down to unbutton my jeans.

"You know, you need to stop," I said, backing up from him.

"All I know is you need to help me get it started. Do you see how you got me?" He said, grabbing the bulge in his jeans. "Baby, please. I'll give you the best ten minutes you ever had in your life, and I promise not to make that much noise. Ten minutes, that's it."

"No. Besides, I'm the one that makes all the noise."

"What if we go in the closet? You can hold on to the rod, and I'll-"

"Are you crazy? What if someone comes in here looking for us, namely your mother?"

"We'll just tell her we're working on those grandbabies she's been hounding us about." He said, pulling me back into his arms.

"Boy, you have lost your mind, and stop that. You know

that's my, my spot."

He had me hooked with one flicker of his tongue. The next thing I knew, our clothes were off, and I was in his favorite position. We had been doing our thing for a good minute when we heard his mother calling our names from the hall.

"We're coming!" He replied.

Literally, he was speaking for the both of us. I was praying she wasn't about to twist that doorknob.

"Well, hurry up. We are getting ready to sit down for dinner!" She shouted.

"Ooh shiii," he let slip.

"Huh?" she asked as I was covering his mouth. Thank God I was on top.

"Nothing, we'll be down, Mother Harris." I said, after finally being able to catch my breath.

"Newlyweds." She mumbled.

"Your mama is going to get you."

"Uh-un, she's gonna get both of us. I wasn't in here by

myself." He said, laughing.

"Well, you started it," I told him.

"Un-huh, and if we don't get out of this bed, I'm about to start round two."

On that note, we both got out of bed to go freshen up.

Chapter 5

BENJAMIN

Momma kind of cut her eyes at me when Tamara and I stood in the line to fix our plates. TJ and Ce laughed and gave each other pounds like they were teenagers in high school at the sight of us. I cleared my throat in an attempt to make them stop because I didn't want them to start Pop up. I knew he had already blessed the food, and us not being there when he did would have been an issue with him.

My mom and aunts knew they put their feet in this food. Since our family was so big, we had several tables that ran from the dining room into the living room. This was one benefit of my parents having such a large home with an open concept. We basically spent every major holiday like this with all of our family and friends together. Some of the ladies in my family would start months in advance to prepare the food by getting their ingredients together, and sometimes, even the men would get in on the action, especially with the barbeques.

At big dinners like this, only the seniors and children were served. For everyone else, it was buffet style, so all you had to do was fix your plate and find a seat. That's just how I liked it. I was able to fill my plate up with a little bit of everything.

After I sat my plate down, I pulled Tamara's chair out for her to sit down. Eight people were at our table, and of course, my table consisted of Ce, TJ, Phillip, myself, and our significant others. Well, sort of because Kherington and Phillip were no longer a couple.

"Nice of you two to join us for dinner," Erica said, grinning.

"It certainly is," Tamara said, laughing.

"That's right, baby. You need to tell her to get some business and to stay out of ours," I said, playfully elbowing Erica.

"Do you think you have enough to eat over there?" Erica asked me.

"Hey, cut him some slack. My boy must've worked up one hell of an appetite." TJ said, causing Ce to slap the table and laugh.

I wasn't thinking about them. I was one lucky man, and my wife was the only one I had to thank for that. She has given me back my life. Ever since this morning, whenever I saw her, I just thank God for her. It was as if I was on a love high, and I had no plans to come down.

She made me feel like rushing through dinner, bypass opening gifts, and speeding home just to be with her again. She was looking sexy, too. She had on a nice black sweater and was wearing the hell out of a pair of jeans. Plus, the thigh-high boots my baby was rocking turned me on. I couldn't help but reach under the table and squeeze her thigh.

Leaning over, I whispered in her ear, "When I get you home, girrrl, I'm going to unwrap you like the gift that you are."

"Is that right?" She giggled.

I was looking at her as if I could put her on a platter and

sop her up with a biscuit. She leaned over to whisper into my ear.

"If you keep looking at me like that, I'm gonna take you down into the basement and make you prove it."

"Girl, don't tempt me. I want you so bad right now, I could turn this damn table over." I whispered back and even tried to get her to touch me, but she snatched her hand back and giggled.

"Do the two of you want to be alone?" Ce asked. "I mean y'all whispering into each other's ears and things. Just let us know so we can go sit at the kiddie table or something."

"Ah, stop it, Ce. I think it's sweet." His new fiancée, Felicia said.

"Thank you, girl. They be hating on me and my man," Tamara said, leaning against me.

"No problem. You know us girls have to stick together."

"I know that's right," Erica added.

"Oh, Lawd, here we go," I sighed.

"What's that supposed to mean, Ben?" Erica asked.

"It means Ce man, get ready for your woman to be corrupted by these two," TJ said, pointing his fingers at both Tamara and Erica.

"Kherington, don't fall into the trap, girl. Promise us that you will stay as far away from these two and their new recruit as possible." I said, noticing how withdrawn she was. Her smile was her only response.

"Girl, you don't have to promise them anything. Come on over to the sweet side," Erica said.

"More like the bitter side," TJ mumbled.

"What was that, Thomas James?" Erica asked.

"Nothing, baby...I wuv you...miss you." He replied, rubbing her back.

"If you wuvved me so much, you would've-"

"Has everyone had enough to eat?" Pop asked in the nick of time. It was clear that Erica was upset with TJ about something. We would have to talk about that a little later.

"Not me, Pop. I'm just making room for dessert," I

replied, with all the kids cheering for dessert behind us.

"Boy, after all you ate, do you have room in there for dessert?"

"Yes, sir. I can never get enough of my momma and aunties cooking."

"We see," he said, and everyone fell out laughing.

Almost everyone had retreated to the great room, to hold his or her own conversation or to look at the game. We were still sitting at the table when I noticed Kherington pretending to be listening to the three stoogettes, Lauretta, Moetta, and Curletta. She appeared to be distant and sad. Which made me wonder if she and Phillip had had another argument prior to coming here. It was plain to see that they weren't on speaking terms.

She was the girl that got away, or should I say, I was too slow to catch. By the time I decided to make my move, Phillip had already beaten me to the punch. I can't help but wonder what if. What if I had asked her out first? Would my life be any better than it was today? I know for sure Stacey wouldn't have been a factor. I would have known of her, but not intimately.

Kherington was something special and different. I've known her since our freshmen year in college, and I've always had a crush on her. It had been a while since we had drinks at Horizons. During our conversation, she asked me if I trusted Phillip with Tamara. I told her I did, only because they had been on business trips alone together, and he hadn't given me a reason not to trust him. But I'd be the first to admit that since she brought them to my attention, I have noticed how attentive Phillip was with Tamara. Seeing how very upset Kherington was last night, and how they were at the party, has me paying closer attention.

There must have been something she picked up on that I missed. I'm interested in knowing what caused her to question me about Phillip. Since she seemed to be uninterested in their conversation, I thought I'd catch up with her in the kitchen, and see what's going on.

"Hey ladies, would any of you be interested in some

red velvet cake?" I asked them. They basically replied no, stating that they had eaten too much already, blah, blah, blah. I reached down and grabbed Kherington's hand, and pulled her up.

"Come on, girl, I know you want some. You've been eyeing that cake plate ever since momma brought it out, now it's gone, but I know there's more in the kitchen."

"Boy, whatever," she said, looking bashful.

She followed me into the kitchen, and surprisingly, there was no one in there but us.

"I know you wanted to get out of there. So what's going on?" I asked.

"I'm good. You know me, little Ms. Rock Steady."

"No. What does that mean?" I sincerely asked her.

"You really want to know? Okay. It's like this, as a woman, I can sometimes be too available, dependable, and loyal. And you'd think a woman like that would have the same things given to her in return, but does Phillip reciprocate the same for me? Let me answer for you, hell no."

"Hey, hey. Where is all of this coming from?" I asked, handing her some tissue from the counter.

"I'm just fed up with all of his crap. He just...I don't know...at this point I'm just really drained."

What concerned me was not what she said, but what could have triggered all of these emotions. In a previous conversation she told me their relationship had ended, and there were no tears then, so why now?

"I'm sorry to hear that you're so unhappy. Had I known, I wouldn't have had you in the same space as Phillip. I get where you're coming from. You already know my situation with this paternity stuff. Do you think if I talked to him that you two could work things out? Or at least be cordial?"

"You know what, Ben? I've often asked myself the same question, but is it worth it? Do you know he has yet to apologize for that display at the Christmas party? Not that he owes me anything, but I was so embarrassed. I left the party because he just stood there, acting as if I wasn't even talking to him. I called him the next day to talk about his blatant disrespect because I knew he wouldn't call me. He didn't care to talk about it then, and he surely doesn't care now. I'm just so tired of being made to feel unwanted." She said with more tears flowing.

"Come here, girl." I pulled her into my arms and held her close. I really felt bad for Kherington.

"Ben, why couldn't he be like you?" She whispered.

At that very moment, I pulled back from her. She stepped closer to me, and slowly, our lips touched as if they were two magnets being pulled together, never to be released.

"Um, um," was the sound that broke our kiss. Only God knows how long we had been kissing.

When I finally opened my eyes, I was glad to see it was TJ. We were still holding each other. Kherington stepped back from me and excused herself. The strange thing is that I really didn't want to let her go.

"Man, what tha hell?" TJ asked, rushing over to me.

"I know. I know."

"What's up with you and Kherington?"

"TJ, I'm telling you it's nothing."

"Nothing? That didn't look like nothing to me. I know you were feeling her from way back, but damn, my boy. Kissing her while your wife is in another room, bro, you wildin'."

"I know, I know. Listen, do you want to lecture me, or do you want the ride of a lifetime?"

"Set her up. Let me see what you've been complaining about, but while you are driving, I'll be listening, too."

"Man, all I want to say about it is this, it didn't mean anything, and my wife is my world, and I'm not messing that up for anybody, dude."

"Un-huh, well, while we're gone, you better hope Erica doesn't catch Tamara and Phillip in the same position; it might be a different story then," he said, holding up the quotation fingers.

"Whateva, man, if you are through with your quotation finger gestures and jokes, let's ride out."

"I'm ready whenever you are, but I'm just saying,
though."

***

Even after getting home, I couldn't help but think of
Kherington. Damn, I'm really tripping. After that mess with
Stacey, I can't afford to look, wonder, or dream about another
woman. But there's something about Kherington that I can't
shake. I can't get over how sweet and soft her lips were. What is
wrong with me?

"What has your mind so captivated over there?" Tamara
asked as she sat in my lap wearing a black lace teddy.

"Right now, at this very moment, you."

"If that were true, why are we still talking?"

"Say less."

From that moment, it was all about Tamara, and she ran
the show.

Chapter 6

STACEY

I was enjoying every moment of being a mother. It was hard work, but I had a great support system. Between my mom, Big Mama, and Jasmine, my baby and I had a tribe that genuinely cared for us. My beautiful baby boy has brought so much joy to me. I never knew I could love like this, and although his father was not currently present in his life, this little boy was going to have everything his heart desired.

Cameron wasn't old enough to even know it was Christmas, but that didn't stop my family from spoiling him rotten. It would take about three cars to get all his stuff home from Big Mama's house. I tried to get Big Mama to let me keep much of it here, but that was a no-go. She said her baby needed all his things. That was code for take all your crap home.

We finally found some quietness when he and I sat alone in the den. Everyone except for mine and Jasmine's family had left Big Mama's house. I had changed, fed, and burped Cameron. He was getting ready to go down for a nap. While he was doing so, I had planned to hit up the kitchen, but when Jasmine walked in, that plan went out of the window.

"Give me my favorite little person. I love me some him. He's such a good baby, Stacey," she said, holding Cameron.

"Yeah, he is. I am truly blessed. With all the drama I went through while carrying him, it's a miracle that he was born healthy." I said, holding his little hand.

"Girl, you're not wrong. Especially with what happened before and after giving birth. Terrance and his wife bomb-rushing you in the hospital wasn't cool, and Ben adding more drama to the mix didn't help."

"Yeah, they did. But at least I know Cameron isn't theirs."

"Speaking of that, I wasn't going to say anything, but I've been watching Cam, and he's starting to look like-"

"Don't even say it. I already know. I noticed it when he

was a week old."

"Girl, what are you going to do?"

"Jas, I don't even know. How do you even explain something like this?"

"Girl, all I know is it's only a matter of time before everyone else starts to notice."

"Tell me about."

"Who would have thought you and him, of all people, hooking up?"

"You know this is all your fault. I blame you for all of this mess."

"Stacey, I know you lying. First of all, I didn't tell you to hop on the magic stick and ride off into the sunset. Don't do that. That was all you, but you must admit, girl, we did have fun that night with all-"

"Hmph, it looks like history has repeated itself. Like mother, like daughter. Another unwedded mother, and the father is nowhere to be found."

"MAMA!" Jasmine shouted.

"Aunt Carmen, you don't know what you're talking about. I know where my child's father is, and if you weren't so busy ear hustling on our conversation, you might have found something better to do with your time."

"I didn't have to ear hustle. You two were talking loud enough for everyone to hear you. I was just on my way in here to ask if you wanted to take some food home since we were breaking everything down in the kitchen."

"And it was mighty convenient of you not to interrupt us, huh? Jas, get your mama. I'm not about to play with her."

"She doesn't have to get me. I'm your elder, and you will respect me."

"What is going on in here?" Big Mama asked.

"Aunt Carmen starting mess, as she always does."

"Carmen, I had to tell you earlier about you and your mouth."

"Mama, these kids are just out of hand and don't show anybody any respect. I had to tell your other grandchildren about the same thing earlier."

"Or is it just you that they don't respect?" I asked.

"See, that right there. That's what I'm talking about."

"What's going on?" Uncle Richard asked. "I can hear you all yelling from the living room."

"Your wife is back here being nosey," I told him.

"Little girl, I told you I wasn't trying to listen to your little conversation. It's not my fault that you don't know where his father is."

I stood to my feet because that was the last straw for me.

"Oh, what are you going to do? Because you are about to get what your mother should have put on your butt years ago. She raised you to be just like her, fatherless and all."

"Carmen! How dare you say that to this child? You, of all people? You have some nerve." Uncle Richard said. "If it weren't for you-" He paused.

"If it weren't for her, what, Daddy?" Jasmine asked.

I sat down when I saw tears run down his face.

"Chantil, would you, Tracey, Keisha, and Jefferson come in here, please?" Big Mama asked.

"Hey, mama, what's wrong?" My mom asked as she looked at the frowning faces in the room.

"It time, baby," she said, grabbing my mother's hand. "It's time to tell them the truth."

My mother looked at my step-father, Uncle Richard, and then Aunt Carmen. "Okay. Girls, can I get you all seated together? We need to talk to you all about something."

"You're not going to tell my children anything!" Aunt Carmen yelled.

"Girls, please," my mom said to Tracey and Keisha, who sat next to Jasmine and me while ignoring her sister. "I know this is going to be difficult and confusing to hear, but we've been keeping a big secret from you all for years."

"I said I didn't want my children to hear this. Girls, let's go," Aunt Carmen demanded.

"Daughters, this is something you all need to hear, and

you will whether your mother wants it told or not. Go ahead, Chantil." Uncle Richard said.

"Before I continue, just know this was a hard, hurtful secret that we kept." My mother said as tears began to roll down her face. My step-father rubbed her back, and Uncle Richard held her hand. It was apparent that she couldn't continue.

"Tracey and Stacey, I am your father. You four are sisters." It was as if someone had sucked all the oxygen out of the room. "I just want you to know I have loved you both and have carried you in my heart as your father from the day I learned of the pregnancy. Your mother and I are not ashamed of how this came to be, but others thought it best to remain a secret. I never wanted it to be this way, and I have lived with years of guilt because of it." He said to us.

"I met your father when I was a freshman at Spelman, and he was just graduating from Morehouse. Our paths crossed at a party. We exchanged numbers and began to get to know one another." Mom said.

"Upon leaving school, I got an opportunity to pastor a church here in Birmingham. We never thought we'd ever see each other ever again." He said.

"I was taking summer courses to get ahead in my studies when I passed out during class. I thought it was from being a little dehydrated from the heat, but as it turned out, I was a few weeks pregnant with you all."

"When your mother phoned me, I was already in a relationship with your Aunt Carmen. It was thought that a young minister having children out of wedlock would go against me. Plus, imagine my shock when learning the two of them were sisters. I had a decision to make, and I chose you two."

"But I told him to have one sister pregnant while dating the other would cause a scandal." Aunt Carmen said.

"So basically, you robbed us of having a father because you cared too much about what others might think of you all?" Tracey asked.

"I would never do that, honey. I was trying to protect

him." She told her.

"Or was it yourself that you were trying to protect?" I asked.

"Stacey, I had nothing to protect myself from."

"Of course you did. He would have done the right the thing by our mother and married her, and you knew that. You didn't want to lose him to her, even if it meant robbing him of a relationship with his children," I told her.

"No, no, that's not it at all. You girls just don't understand. It was a different time back then."

"No, Aunt Carmen, what we understand is the loss of not knowing our father and the feeling of abandonment," I said, crying.

Chapter 7

BENJAMIN

I still can't get Kherington off of my mind. Kissing her on Christmas Day was one thing, but having her over to the house for New Year's Eve was something different. I could feel the tension between us and desperately hoped no one else could pick up on our vibes. We didn't say much to one another, but the continued glances we gave each other was far too much to ignore. In other words, if we were alone, there was no telling what might have happened between us. I needed someone to talk to about this.

I couldn't talk to TJ's stupid butt because he would advise me to go after her, and I damn sure couldn't talk to Phillip. That only leaves me with two options: Ce or Pop. I didn't want to hear a sermon on 'thou shalt not commit adultery,' but Ce was in court, and I needed help now.

I pulled into an empty parking spot right next to Pop's. It

was Saturday morning, and I knew he would be here preparing for tomorrow.

"Hey, Pop, did I catch you at a bad time?"

"Oh no, son, I'll always make time for my boys, despite what your mother used to say."

"Good, 'cause I have a problem."

"What kind of problem?" He asked with concern.

"Well, it's like this. There is this woman that I've liked for years, and we kind of shared an intimate moment."

"Intimate moment?"

"Yeah, um, we've kissed once and have recently seen each other, but nothing outside the norm has happened. She's someone that I consider to be a friend."

"Okay." He said, sitting back in his chair.

"So here's my problem. I can't get her out of my mind. I dreamt of the day that we could be together, and now, I don't know. I mean, I know that I am married, of course, and she was dating a mutual friend, but I can't stop thinking about her, Pop. If

I don't do something about these thoughts or feelings, I don't know what's going to happen."

"What about your wife?"

"What about her? She's there. We are going through some things but trying to work it out."

"If you are trying to make things work with your wife, why are you thinking about another woman? Your focus should be on the one you stood before God and countless others and promised to love and honor for better or worse, not until something better comes along."

"I hear what you're saying, Pop, but I can't stop thinking about my friend."

"Well, let me put it to you in a way I know you can understand. What if Tamara were sitting where you are and she said, 'I can't stop thinking about this other man, and if nothing changes, then I don't know what I'm going to do?' How would you feel?"

"To be truthfully honest, Pop, I would be devastated. I

would feel like a fool for working so hard on putting our relationship back together, only to have her leave me, anyway."

"So, as you can see, there is more at stake than thinking of someone. If you decide to act on your thoughts or feelings, just remember that you have four individuals involved in this."

"Four individuals, like who?"

"You and the other woman, you and your wife, you and the guy she's dated, and last but not least, you and God."

There was nothing I could say behind that.

"So the question is, do you want your marriage?"

"Yeah, Pop. I love my wife and want my marriage."

"If you love her so much, why hurt her in this way? I understand that this woman was someone you liked years ago, but if it were meant for you two to be together, it would have happened then, not now, not like this. Let the past stay in the past, son. You have a second chance at happiness with your wife that you so-call love. It would be my wish that everyone who got married stayed that way for the rest of their lives. But I understand because of certain circumstances, it does not always happen that way. My advice to you, son, would be to seek marriage counseling; that way, you can talk to your wife about the thoughts you're having in a safe space and perhaps why you are having them. The reason I say this is that you told me that you were thinking of your friend, but you never mentioned why. Is it because you love her or are you lusting after her?"

"I think it's because she's the one that got away. I may never know what my life could have been with her."

"So you would risk destroying your marriage over a what if?"

"No, I just wanted to know what it would be like, and I also know she's having a hard time in her current relationship with our mutual friend, and that made me feel some sorta way towards her."

"And you would rather destroy your marriage because you feel this person's pain?"

"No, Pop, I'm not saying that. I just, I don't know," I said in frustration.

"Son, be careful. That's temptation that you're dealing with, and if you are not careful, you will end up losing what you know and love, Tamara. Every man faces temptation in one way or another, but practicing self-discipline will prevent you from falling. Temptation is everywhere. I, myself, have been tempted to do the wrong thing, but do you know what stops me? Me. I never want to know a day that I intentionally hurt my wife because of infidelity. I'm just telling you about me and mine. God has blessed us with too many good years together to do something so reckless. My thoughts and prayers are with you, son."

"Thanks, Pop."

"Anytime. I love you, son. Remember what I said, now."

I left Pop's office with a new mindset. He had advised me to let go of the past because I couldn't relive yesterday. But what I knew that Pop didn't was I had already cheated on Tamara mentally, and because of that, I had already put Kherington before her. She was the first thing I thought about in the morning and the last thing I thought about before going to bed. Tamara, on the other hand, hadn't noticed the change. Because if she had known that I was thinking of some other woman, she would've skyed up out of our marriage before I could change my mind good. Pop had me thinking. What if it was the other way around? I'd probably go ballistic.

I was so disturbed by the mere thought of it that I almost dropped my cellphone when I tried to answer it. I'm glad that I was stopped at a traffic light.

Speak of the devil. "Hello."

"Hey, are you busy?" She asked.

"No, ah, what's up?" She had never called before. Why was she calling me now?

"I just wanted to talk to you."

"Oh, okay. Well, you have my undivided attention. What's going on?"

"Well, I was thinking maybe we could have a drink

together later on at Horizons."

"That's fine. Hopefully, Phillip won't mind. He'll most likely be there, if that's okay?"

"Forget him. That's who I mostly wanted to talk to you about."

"What time do you want to meet? I have a few errands to run?" I told her.

"Two is good for me? What about you?"

"That'll be great. See you soon."

"Bye."

Chapter 8

KHERINGTON

I could have just kicked myself for not breaking up with

Phillip sooner. I knew from day one that Ben was a better man

for me than Phillip. I was the envy of all the girls on campus, but

look at me now. Now, I wished Ben had asked me out first. He

was the total opposite of Phillip. Even though I had heard of his

playboy ways, I knew Ben was different. All he needed was the

right woman on his side, and I should have been her. Had I

known then what I know now, Ben and I would have been

happily married with children. He wouldn't have put his needs

before mine and emotionally abandoned me. No, Ben wouldn't

have done that, not like that bastard Phillip had. Even now he is

concerned about me and I him. We talked mainly about our

relationship issues. I'll never forget when Ben was down about

possibly losing his marriage because of an outside child, and

how happy he was to learn the woman was having a boy. I just know he'd make a great father.

I'd never stopped liking Ben, even when Phillip and I were just getting to know each other. The only other reason I talked to Phillip over Ben was because of Terrilyn McCoy, a girl I despised. She was head over heels in love with Phillip. She and I were rivals. We competed in everything from academics to our individual sororities. I hated that girl with a passion. Every time you saw her, she was in her sorority paraphernalia. She wore something red just about everyday. Walking around talking about she was the real McCoy and not like some of these wannabes, of course, talking about me. So when I heard that Phillip had dumped her butt, I knew that was my time to shine. I purposely swayed my hips from side to side to get his attention every time I saw him. Just as my luck would have it, I was leaving out of my biology class when I saw Phillip standing there listening to Terrilyn whine about him not calling her. So, I conveniently walked up to them and handed him a flyer for my sorority's party.

"Ah, excuse you, but I know you see us talking," the witch said, rolling her eyes at me.

"All I see is you talking and him not listening," I said, returning my attention to him. "So, will you be there tonight?" I asked him sweetly.

"There's no other place me and the fellas would rather be." He said, taking the flyer with that sexy smile of his.

"I can think of a few other places. Now, if you are finished with this lame-ass invite, I would like to continue my conversation," the helfa said.

"You're right about one thing, Terrilyn. We are finished," he said to her. "Kherington, can I walk you to your next class?" He asked me.

"Sure," I replied. To make her even madder, I purposely held his hand as we walked away, leaving her standing there looking stupid.

Later that night, Terrilyn and her entourage decided to crash our party. That helfa really wanted to fight me over

Phillip's no-good butt. I couldn't believe it. I don't think I had ever been called out my name so many times in all my life. She thought she was going to confront Phillip and me together, but he never showed.

Now, I wish I had left well enough alone. I should've minded my own business and gone on to class. Terrilyn ended up married and having three children to my nothing. All I have are my best friends and parents. A guilt trip kept Phillip and me together for years, but proof of him not caring about anyone but himself has freed me.

Chapter 9

PHILLIP

I was getting ready to go hang out at Horizons. Lately, some fresh faces had been coming through, and I was enjoying the scenery. I was just about to put my shoes on when my phone rang. Looking at the caller ID, I knew I shouldn't have answered, but that would mean possibly having to talk to her later, since she and Ben are so Buddy Buddy, so what the hell?

"Yeah?" I answered.

"Is that the way we answer the phone now?" She asked with a ton of attitude.

I knew I shouldn't have answered the damn phone.

"Yes, I was getting-"

"Well, we need to talk."

"Like I was saying before you interrupted me, I was getting ready to go out. So, can this wait until tomorrow?"

"No. This is more important. She can wait."

"She who? What's so important that it can't wait? I told-"

"What it concerns is us."

"Okay," I said, like that made a difference.

"I have packed up whatever items you left over here, and will send them to you," she said.

Wow, I never thought I'd hear her say those words. I wanted her to reach this point a few years ago, but she wouldn't let go and kept fighting me on it.

"Thank you, Kherington. I want you to know that I have nothing but respect for you and-"

"If you respected me so much, why was it so hard for you to commit to me?"

"It was nothing wrong with you. It was me. I told you I wasn't ready for the type of relationship you wanted." I lied. It was most definitely her.

"How long have you known that you weren't ready?"

Again, with this, I answered. "Since the beginning."

"Why then allow us to go on this long, wasteful journey with so much pain if you didn't want to be in a serious relationship with me? I had options.”

“Kherington, I told you I wasn’t looking for anything serious even then. You were so hell-bent on, I mean, you were so focused on trying to change my mind that time just passed.” I said, switching up my wording to keep calm. I’ve been down this road too many times not to know her angle. She won’t be able to cry victim today.

“Why not just break it off? Why keep me holding on?”

“Why didn’t you? I tried to break it off, but you guilt-tripped me back into it. To be very honest, the day you found out that you were pregnant, I was planning on calling it quits, but when you told me, the only thing I could think about was not being ready to be a father.”

“Selfish as usual, Phillip.”

“That may be true, but how selfish are you to keep a relationship going because of a grudge? See, you are quick to point fingers and find fault, but you are also to blame.”

“Well, foolish me thought she had a real man in her life,

and unfortunately, I misjudged you."

"You knew exactly what you were getting into when you decided to keep seeing me."

"Yeah, and I wasted eight whole years of my life for nothing. To say I have a newfound hatred for you is an understatement."

"That's too bad because I don't hate you. I wish you nothing but the best out of life." I told her before she hung up on me.

Kherington had no reason to come at me like that. I was upfront and honest with her from day one. It was she that wanted more than I was willing to give. I had my heart broken once, and I promised myself that I would never allow that to happen to me again. My casual date with Kherington lasted eight years. I can't front and say I didn't have feelings for her, they just weren't the same as hers or the way she needed them to be. Unfortunately, Kherington was not the woman I saw myself spending the rest of my life with. That woman was already taken, if only she and I had met in a different place in time.

Chapter 10

BENJAMIN

I guess it's just me tonight. Tam went out with Erica and TJ was spending time with JJ. Ce is somewhere romancing Felecia, and Phillip was on his way to Horizons. I may as well join him, since I had nothing else better to do. I wanted to talk to him about Kherington. Speaking of her, she was calling me.

"Hello, gorgeous."

"Hey." she said, smiling through the phone. "What are you doing?"

"Nothing. I was just thinking about what I could get into tonight. What's up with you?"

"Phillip and I had it out, and I'm a little down."

"I'm sorry to hear that, Kheri. What can I do to help?"

"If you don't mind being a listening ear, I wouldn't mind accepting your company."

Everything in me was shouting, **"NO"** don't go.

"Sure, can I bring you anything?"

"Thanks, but I'm good. I'm sending you my address. See you soon."

I kept telling myself that I was going to her house for moral support. As I headed down the highway, I kept hearing Pop's voice telling to me to turn around, but I couldn't. My relationship with Kherington was purely platonic. Talking to Pop made me realize that I had more at stake than my hormones. No way was I going to ruin my marriage and business fooling around.

I parked my car in front of Kherington's house. Not a single light was on, but her car was in the driveway. There goes that voice again. This time, it was more persistent than ever. I brushed off the warning and proceeded toward her front door.

I rang the doorbell and waited for her to answer. Finally, after the second ring, she opened the door. I couldn't really see her because it was so dark inside. I wouldn't have known it was her if it weren't for the streetlight.

"Are you going to cut on some lights?"

"No." she said softly.

"I know we should conserve energy, but this is a little much. I can hardly see my hand in front of my face."

"Follow me." She said, pulling me further into the house.

"Follow you where? Girl, I can't even see you."

She continued to pull me in the direction she wanted me to go. I was starting to feel a little uneasy.

Suddenly, we stopped walking. I could see a little glow of light coming from the end of what I could only assume was a hall. What concerned me the most was the need for all the secrecy and darkness. What kind of game was she playing?

"Okay, we stopped walking, but why?"

"Because I want to give you something."

"Give me something. Something like what? Whatever it is, please let me see it with the lights on."

"Sorry, I won't be able to do that." She said seductively.

"And why not?" I said, starting to become even more concerned. "Kherington, I don't know about you, but this is starting to make me feel a little uncomfortable, and I think I should just..."

That was all I was able to say before she put her soft lips on mine. Without breaking our kiss, she slowly walked backward into this room. Once there, I saw that the room was all aglow with candles, and that's when I made the best discovery of them all. Standing before me was a naked Kherington. When we were kissing, she held my hands away from her body. Had I known she was naked when she opened the door, I would have made an about-face. Now that I can see everything, it was clear what I should do, but my feet wouldn't move.

"So, do you like your gift?" She asked, twirling around.

Eying her up and down, I replied. "What is there not to like? I can't say that I will be enjoying your present."

"I'm sorry, maybe you misunderstood. It's not just a gift, but gifts. As in more than one." She said, letting her hair fall loose.

"Ah, Kherington," I said, with a lump in my throat. I was breaking into a sweat and trying hard to fight the feeling that stirred in me. "I can't sleep with you."

"You're right. You won't be sleeping with me," she said, now standing a breath away. "However, I will be sleeping with you," she told me.

When she kissed me again, I lost all self-control and fell captive to her spell and I knew then that I was in trouble.

***

Chapter 11

BENJAMIN

"Man, TJ, where are you?" I asked after calling him twice.

"On my way to tha house. What's up?"

"I need an alibi."

"An Alibi? For what? And please don't tell me you messin' with Stacey again?"

"Hell no!" I screamed through the phone. I didn't mean to yell, but instead of him listening, he was asking questions. "TJ, listen, I just left Kherington's house and-"

"You left whose house?"

"Kherington's man, but-"

"What the hell you doing over there? Aww, snap! You hit, dawg?" He whispered, "You did, didn't you?"

I swear I'm about to go off. I needed him to focus and listen to me so that we could have our stories straight. "Dude, I need you to vouch for me. We were at Horizons all night, alright?"

"Sho. But tell me, how was it?" I could hear him grinning through the phone, showing all 32 teeth.

"She was insatiable. TJ, when I tell you, man, she has messed my mind up. I don't know what the hell Phillip was thinking, but if she were mine, I would be on a Gatorade ginseng protein diet. Man, she worked me out!"

"Ooooo. And see, you didn't even want to get at her."

"I know. It just sorta happened."

"To look at her, you wouldn't think she got down like that," TJ said.

"All I can say is she's a beast in them sheets. From the time I got there until my leaving, it was own."

"So now what?" He asked.

"Nothing."

"Get the hell out of here. You mean to tell me after hitting that you're not going to tap that again?"

"That's exactly what I'm telling you," I answered.

"If you say so, but I doubt it. She's got you open."

"I don't think so. I always wanted to know how it would be to have her in that way, and now that I know, I have no reason to go back. I promised myself that I wouldn't mess up my marriage, and I'm not. I know it sounds ass-backwards, but I love my wife, and no sneaky link, no matter how good she was, is going to change that."

"Aight, man. You know, I say that same thing about Erica. Even though we're not married, I still get an itch from time to time."

"Time to time. You mean like every other day."

"But, I no longer scratch the itch. That's what I'm trying to tell you. You know I got you. I'll be your alibi. I talked to Erica earlier. She said that they were having a girl's night out and would be going to dinner and a movie."

"Cool. We are home free then. They'll be asleep when we both get there."

"That's what I know. Erica will pick up JJ tomorrow, and

while she's out, you can come over and tell me every kinky detail about your evening."

"I'm not telling you anything. I think you're a little too involved in it, as is."

"No, sir. I need some details. I've been waiting on y'all to hook up for the longest, and now you don't have nothing to say."

I laughed at his comment. "But that doesn't mean I have to put her business out there like that."

"Tomorrow around three, be here." That was the last thing he said, and in good time, too, because now I was home, pulling into my garage.

I eased into the house, walking as softly as I could. I made it upstairs without the slightest sound. Once I entered our bedroom, I found Tamara sound asleep. I jumped into the shower to wash off Kherington's scent and my indiscretion. After drying off and dressing, I eased into our bed, shifted until I found a comfortable spot, and closed my eyes.

"Where have you been?" Tamara asked, groggy.

"Hey, sweetheart," I said, kissing her on the forehead. "I was at Horizons. Did you enjoy your evening?"

"Un-huh."

"Hey, it's late. I'm going to get some sleep. I told TJ I would see him later on today," I said in between yawns. The next thing I knew, I had fallen asleep.

Chapter 12

TAMARA

Ben's explanation of where he was didn't set well with me because it was a flat out lie. I called Erica to see if TJ's lying butt was going to say the same thing.

"Did you ever ask TJ where he was last night?"

"Yeah, but he didn't go into any details."

"Ben told me they were at Horizons all night."

"I don't understand how that was even possible when we were there till midnight."

"Exactly, I even asked Joe, the bartender, if he had seen him," I said.

"Yeah, I remember that, and he said no."

"I knew Ben had lied, but I didn't let on. My biggest fear is that he had started back messing around with Stacey." I told Erica.

"Girl, I hope not. She's done enough."

"Yeah, but she hadn't contacted Ben at all, to my knowledge. So it may not be her."

"Good, I wonder how she's doing now since she's had the baby and not being able to come and go like she once did."

"According to Lisa, her grandmother and mom has her son more than she does. They loved that little boy. I know Terrance is glad that he dodged that bullet. If he were the father, he'd probably never see him." I told her.

"I know he is relieved, but-"

"But what about Ben? I already know Erica. He hadn't said two words to me about that either. I hope Stacey's not thinking that I'm keeping him from the baby."

"Why make the baby pay for her mistakes? He didn't ask to be here." She said.

"I wouldn't. I have nothing to do with any of it. He just should be glad that she didn't have twins."

"Twins?"

"Yeah, I didn't tell you Stacey was a twin?"

"You mean to tell me it's two of them running around here?"

"Yes. Lisa said Stacey's twin is the total opposite of her."

"Well, thank God for small favors because the world wouldn't have been ready for two of them."

"I know that's right. Nobody's man would be safe."

"Hey, Tam, let me call you right back. I'm pulling up to pick up JJ. I'll call you when I get him home and settled."

"Sure," I told Erica and hung up the phone.

As soon as I did, my mind went right back to Ben. I just don't understand why he would lie about where he was last night. I thought we were over and beyond keeping secrets from one another, and here we are, right back at square one.

Chapter 13

ERICA

Tamara and I both had our work cut out for us. Our men stayed out until the wee hours of the morning and they were lying about their whereabouts. Hopefully, Tamara and I can put our heads together and figure this out. We already know they lied, but what was eating me was why. I had my own theory of where TJ was, but Ben was a different story.

"Hey, Tam, I'm back."

"You know, Erica, this is really bothering me. After all we've been through, he has the nerve to lie to me again. Unbelievable."

"I understand where you are coming from. I have a little haunch of my own about where TJ was. My instincts are pointing me in one direction. Hold on and don't say a word."

"Alright."

I clicked over to call the only place TJ would have been

last night. After Christmas, I made it plainly clear to him that I didn't want him over there unless it was necessary.

"Tam," I said, connecting us on a three-way call.

"Yeah." she whispered.

"Okay, remember, don't say anything."

We both sat there in silence while the other line rang.

"Hello."

"Hi, Jasmine. How are you doing?"

"I'm fine, just a little tired."

"I didn't mean to disturb you. I was just checking to see if our little man had eaten lunch already. I forgot to ask you when I picked him up."

"He slept in this morning and had a late breakfast. So he might not be hungry."

"A late breakfast?"

"Yeah, he and his father thought it was a good idea to drive me crazy and make noise all night long."

"Really?" TJ was busted. "What time did Jay go to bed?

Keeping that baby up all night, TJ should be ashamed of himself."

"It was pretty late. That's why he was napping when you picked him up. When the baby comes, they won't be making all that noise. You can believe that."

"Baby? What baby? I didn't know you were seeing anyone." I was glad to have been sitting down because hearing that would have knocked me down.

"Oh girl, you know how it is." She said slyly.

"How far along are you?" I asked without agreeing.

"Three months today."

"Congratulation. Now, I know why you are so tired."

"Thank you. That and I didn't go to bed until one this morning because we were talking about putting JJ in preschool."

"That's awesome. If you need any help selecting a good school, just let me know. I don't mind helping."

"I will. I was just telling TJ we needed to ask you about it last night, or was that early this morning, but anyway? We will."

I didn't particularly appreciate how she said early this morning, as if she was throwing something in my face. And why hadn't he mentioned her pregnancy? "He hadn't mentioned it yet, but I'll start a list of good schools for you all. Our little party animal is up and playing now."

"You just don't know how much I looked forward to you picking him up so that I could take this nap."

"Trust me, I know," I said dryly. "Well, get your rest. Goodbye." I said, hanging up the phone before she could respond.

After making sure the line was cleared, I asked, "Girl, did you hear that?"

"Yes, I did. Word for word." Tam said.

"I wonder if TJ knows she is pregnant because he hasn't said anything to me."

"Maybe not. I know one thing for sure, half of this mystery has been solved."

"Yeah, it has, but it doesn't mean my situation is any

better than yours. I told TJ's ass that he should only go over to her house to pick Jay up, and that's it. I'm still pissed off about Christmas Eve." I told her.

"Now, I'm more worried than before because this means he wasn't with TJ at all. So where in the hell was he last night?"

"I wish I knew where to begin with that one, Tam. I have a couple of chores to do before making Jay some lunch. I'll call you a little later."

"Okay, talk to you soon. Bye."

I feel bad now. If I hadn't included her on the call, she would probably give Ben a second chance to come clean. Not only does she know he wasn't at Horizons, but he wasn't with TJ either. I would have thought for sure he would never jeopardize his marriage, but obviously, Tam and I both have been fooled.

Chapter 14

STACEY

It's been about a few weeks or so since the big secret, and I still can't believe the man Tracey and I once knew, as our uncle was actually our father. After I spoke what I felt like was the truth, nothing but tears followed. Tracey held me, and he pulled us into his arms as we all cried together. I do not believe, with the exception of Cameron and Aunt Carmen, that there was a dry eye in the room.

Through the years, our father had looked out for us as he did Jasmine and Keisha, but it wasn't the same. To know him as dad would have meant the world to us. When we later found out that our other uncles and aunts knew about it, too. That made the situation even worse. How could they keep a secret like that away from us?

He wanted to meet with Tracey and me over dinner sometime next week, and we accepted his invitation. It would just be the three of us because I guess he knew with everything being out in the open, Aunt Carmen wasn't one of our favorite people, especially not mine. It was bad blood between us, and there was no way I would ever forgive her. But who she hurt the most was Tracey. She loved Aunt Carmen. Our aunt even tried to call Tracey to apologize, but after realizing she wouldn't answer or return any of her phone calls, she sent her a long text message instead.

This secret has caused a devastating blow in my immediate family, so much so that Jasmine and I haven't spoken. I never thought there would ever come a day that we wouldn't speak. Even as little girls, we were inseparable. Our family was wild and crazy, but nothing like this had ever happened. How do I explain this to Cameron? I was starting to get a headache just from the thought when my phone rang.

"Well, it's about damn time!" I yelled into the phone.

"Hey," she said.

"Hey? Where have you been?" I asked her.

"I thought maybe you needed some time and space to process everything. I know I did, and to be honest, I'm still at a loss."

"Jas, no matter what is going on, we're blood, and nothing will change that. I love you, girl. We were supposed to be over here figuring things out together."

"I love you, too. I, I just, I don't know. We are sisters, Stacey."

"Yeah, I know. How's Keisha handling everything?"

"You know her. She's mad at the world instead of placing the blame where it belongs."

"I get it."

"And to make matters worse, our parents aren't speaking to one another," Jasmine said.

"All of this secrecy has caused so much drama," I replied.

"I guess, but hiding it made things that much worse."

"True, but what can we do? Tracey and I missed out on something we could only dream about."

"We have each other now. I know you all will be having dinner with dad next week. I wish I could be there, but I understand that he wanted to spend time alone with you all. But you know what, Stacey, I'm glad it's out. Do you remember when the four of us would go places with him, and he'd introduce us as his girls?"

"I remember that! He'd always call us that. It made me feel so special."

"Maybe in dad's own way, he was letting things be known."

"Maybe so, but we can't rewrite the past. We can only move forward."

"Speaking of moving forward, when are you going to talk to Cam's father? We know how keeping things in the dark destroys families."

"I will call him. I'm just searching for the right words. This is difficult."

"Yeah, I know. All I can say is to be honest. He'll be

angry, but at least he'll know about his child."

"You're right, Jas, and I'll speak to him soon."

"Have you heard from him?"

"He sent me a Merry Christmas text but nothing else," I told her.

"Mmm, do you think he knows?"

"I can't see how. You're the only one that noticed any-" I paused to see who was calling me on the other line. "Hey, let me call you back. This is Ben calling me."

"Okay."

"Bye."

Chapter 15

BENJAMIN

"Hello."

"Hi, Stacey. Did I catch you at a bad time?"

"No. How can I help you?" She asked, being very short.

"I was calling to speak with you about getting a paternity test done for Cameron?"

"There's no need. You are not his father."

"How do you know?" I asked.

"Believe me, you are not."

"Believe you like Terrance believed you?"

"I take it you are aware that he, too, is not the father of Cameron?"

"Yes, I am aware. That's why I wanted to take the paternity test." I said, becoming frustrated.

"But there's no reason for you to do that. He is not your son, Benjamin."

"I hear you, but I'd rather know for myself that he is not than to take your word for it."

"Do what you have to do. It's not like you won't, anyway. Is this the reason I keep getting these random phone calls about setting up an appointment for a paternity test? Because they need to stop, now."

"Stacey, I don't know what your problem is, or why you have an attitude towards me, but I haven't had anyone to contact you. It, however, doesn't seem like a bad idea to make the appointment. All I'm trying to do is what is right for Cameron."

"What is right, huh? Where was all this righteousness weeks ago? My son is almost three months old. The last time I saw or even heard from you was right after giving birth, and now you want to do what's right? Suddenly, you have time to talk about it now. No, how are you guys doing? Merry Christmas? Can I get you anything? Do you need anything? Not a single word from you. So when you do call, I'm supposed to jump over backward to honor your request? I don't think so."

"Stacey, I understand, and I apologize for not being there for you all, but this situation has turned my life literally upside down."

"Well, luckily for you, he is not your son."

"You don't know that!"

"Yes, I do! And for the last time, Benjamin, Cameron is not your son."

"Unless you have proof that he belongs to someone else, it'll be in my best interest to have this test done."

"It's all about you, isn't it? I thank God that you're not his father. He has one, so please go live your perfect little life with your wife, and leave me and mine the hell alone." She said before hanging up the phone.

Stacey had never spoken to me in that way. I couldn't say a single word. She was right. I had not checked on them or anything. I was so busy trying to save my marriage that I simply forgot. What kind of father could I be to forget about his child? I don't know if I am more disturbed by her saying Cameron wasn't mine or by the way she spoke to me. Either way, it hurt.

Chapter 16

KHERINGTON

Just the person I've been waiting to hear from.

"Hello."

"Hello, Ms. Draker. This is William. I have completed my assignment, and it's being emailed to you as we speak."

"Thank you, William. I am sure what you found is worth every penny it cost me to gather this information."

"Of course, and you will also receive pictures, as promised. You know how to reach me if you ever need my services again."

"Thank you so much. I just received the report with photos. Excellent work, William, as always."

"Thank you, Ms. Draker. Until next time."

***

I printed the report and started to read it with a glass of wine. What have you been up to, Mr. Gray? Phillip, Phillip,

Phillip. The many games you play. To think I was once in love with you. Hiring William to follow Phillip months ago was the best thing I had ever done. I should've done this a long time ago. Maybe if I had, I wouldn't have to tie up these loose ends. I was desperate for information. I wanted to know what was keeping him from committing to me. Just as I feared, it was not what was keeping him but whom, as I am now, finding out.

My heart was breaking, not because of him cheating or from any kind of abuse, but because I was never loved the way he loves her. He loved her from afar. Phillip is nurturing with her. Where was my love and tender care through the years? He truly cares for her in a way I could only imagine. Now, he knows how it feels to love someone incapable of loving him back. It doesn't feel so good, does it, Phillip? Finally, I get to see him suffer as I did. I thought as a looked at their photo together.

Chapter 17

ERICA

It was our weekend with JJ, and he was full of energy after waking up from his nap. He was running around pulling out every toy he owned, eating sliced apples, and talking my head off. I was so into my baby registry that I had completely tuned him out until he called my name.

"Mommy Erica?"

"Yes, Sweetie."

"Are you gonna love momma and daddy new baby like me?" He asked so innocently.

I was taken aback. Did I hear him correctly? "I'm sorry, sweetheart. What did you say?"

"Me, mommy and daddy, new baby?"

"Your mommy and daddy are having a baby?" I asked. I had just turned down his favorite cartoon to hear him clearly.

"Un-huh."

"Finish eating your apples," I told him as I sat back in

disbelief on the sofa.

Oh my God. I have to calm down. I couldn't let JJ see me

this way. I was so upset that I went upstairs and called Tamara.

"Tam, I hope you got my damn bail money, girl, because

I'm about to kill this son of a bi-"

"Erica! What's wrong? What are you talking about?"

"Jay just told me his mommy and daddy are having a new

baby."

"HE SAID WHAT!?"

"Yes, and as soon as TJ comes back here, it is going to be

on and popping."

"Wait a minute, you don't want to do anything out of

anger. We only have one part of the story. It would help if you

had the truth, and the only way to get that is from TJ. I just pray

he tells it."

"Somehow, Tam, whether it's the truth or a lie, it will all

hurt the same. I'll talk to you later." I said, hanging up the phone.

I was in a confused daze. "Please, Lord, let this all be a big misunderstanding." I prayed while sitting on my bed.

"Mommy Erica, don't cry. I will bring you some tissues and a Band-Aid, okay?"

I hadn't realized I was crying until JJ climbed up in my lap. He was such a sweetheart. He's never given me any trouble.

"Okay, Mommy Erica, here is your tissue, now where is your boo boo?" He asked.

"I didn't hurt myself, sweetie. I'm just sad."

"Oh. Where do you put the Band-Aid if you are sad?"

"Good question."

"You're crying again. Do you want me to get you some more tissue?"

"No, sweetheart. I'll be okay," I told him, knowing that was the farthest from the truth.

"Don't be sad. I love you, okay?" He told me, holding my face and then hugging my neck tightly.

"Thank you, I needed that."

Chapter 18

TJ

"My guy! What's good with you?" I asked Ben.

"Man, I can't call it. What's good with you?"

"Work as usual. I'm trying to get everything ready for when the baby comes."

"Yeah, we don't have long. How's Erica been doing?" He asked.

"She's good. I haven't checked in on her and JJ yet, but I will in a few."

"That's good. I haven't heard from Tamara all day. I should check on her, too."

"What about our other friend? Are you going to check on her also?" I asked, laughing.

"I'm trying to stay as far away from that as humanly possible. To be honest with you, we haven't spoken since that night."

"You know how busy Kherington is. Being a pathologist, the hospital keeps her busy."

"True, but what would I say even if we did talk? I mean, I couldn't tell her how I truly feel."

"Why not?"

"Because it would be inappropriate."

"How does telling someone how you feel about them become inappropriate?"

"Because a married man shouldn't have these thoughts and feelings for someone other than his wife."

"Man, you got it bad."

"In the worst way." He confessed.

"What are you going to do about it?"

"Place my attention where it should be, on my wife."

"I hear you, man. Handle your business. Hey, I'm about to check on the family. Hit me up a little later."

"One." He said before hanging up.

I wouldn't want to be in his shoes for nothing in the

world. I thought as I called Erica.

"Hey, baby mama. What are you and JJ doing?"

"I hear you have another baby on the way?"

"Excuse me! What are you talking about?"

"You heard me! And you better be glad that he's in the other room, or you'd be getting cursed out right now."

"Erica. I have no idea what you're talking about."

"Oh, really? Well, according to JJ, you and Jasmine are having another baby."

"Me and who? No ma'am. Jasmine and I aren't having anything together."

"Well, she is pregnant?"

"Who told you that?"

"She did. She's three months."

"Wait a minute. She's what?"

"Three months."

"By who?"

"According to JJ, you."

"Hold on a sec." I placed Erica on hold and called Jasmine.

"Hello." She answered.

"Jasmine, why is your son at my house starting trouble?"

"What do you mean?"

"Man, he don' told Erica that his mama and daddy were having a baby."

"No, we ain't either! That child of mine. He asked me with his nosey self why my belly was so big, and I told him because I was having a baby like his daddy was having a baby, and he must have put the two together. You saw your life flash before your eyes, didn't you?" She asked, laughing,

"Man, I was afraid to go home. Erica is on the call, too. I had to call you because she wasn't going to believe a word that I said. I bet my stuff is outside right now?"

"He's telling the truth this time, Erica." She said, still laughing.

"Congratulations and thank you!" I told her.

"Bye, y'all." She said.

"Un-huh, now say you are sorry for accusing me."

"Nope, because you lied about where you were a few weeks ago."

"Come on, Erica."

"Goodbye." She said, hanging up on me.

Man, I must be slipping. How was I going to get out of this without exposing Ben?

Chapter 19

TAMARA

I was sitting at my favorite table in the back of my new getaway spot. This was the coffee shop Marcus and I met at when I told him there could be nothing between us. He went inside, and I left. The following week, I returned and went inside, hoping to bump into him. While there, I had a chance to enjoy the cozy ambiance and friendly staff. I can see why Marcus would choose this place. It had a romantic feel to it. If I had entered inside, who knows what my decision would have been?

I ordered my usual caramel macchiato with extra caramel and an apple-cinnamon muffin. This place allowed me room to indulge in something good and filter through my thoughts, and boy did I have plenty of them. I just saw the sweetest couple walk in and they made me smile. I remember how that was once Ben and me, but look at us now.

Turmoil after turmoil, relationship after relationship, one misguided decision after the next. When will it all end? Having Ben confront me with the kiss in the elevator with Marcus was one thing, but sleeping with Phillip was diabolical. And although Phillip and I haven't dared to repeat our heinous act, it still lingered in the back of my mind if what we had done somehow leaked out. Could this be the reason why Ben lied about his whereabouts, and since somehow finding out, he has started back seeing Stacey? This was driving me crazy. I was tired of wondering and needed answers. There was only one person that could feed my curiosity. I never thought I'd be dialing this number again, but here I am.

"Hello."

"Hello, Stacey. This is Tamara. How are you?"

"I'm a little busy at the moment. Newborns, you know." She said, agitated.

"I apologize for the interruption. Can you give me a call when you're free? I really need to talk to you about something."

"Talk to me about what? Look, as I told your husband, who probably has put you up to calling me because I've blocked him, Cameron is not his son. So, he can stop having that damn lab call me about taking a paternity test."

"Stacey, Ben, does not know anything about me contacting you, and I'm unaware of anyone calling you from a lab," I told her.

"Oh. Well, I still don't know what it is you could possibly want to talk to me about. What happened between Ben and I is water under the bridge. If anything, I feel sorry for you."

"Sorry for me?" I asked taken aback.

"Yes. You are married to a narcissistic manipulator. Once he has had his fill of you or becomes bored with you, you will be replaced. That's what happened to me when he met you."

"But you were engaged to his brother and seeing other people," I said, running back all the things he had said about her versus what I already knew. "He told me the two of you weren't serious. That it was pretty much a casual thing, and you didn't want it to end."

"Did he also tell you on that faithful day that we slept together before he broke things off? He controlled everything about our relationship. He made me feel special by sweeping me off of my feet. This trip, that trip, this gift, that gift, the wining and dining, he did it all. He even gave me the down payment for my townhouse and wanted to buy me a car. Does any of that sound casual to you? Then, when he was done with me, I was of no further use." She said.

"I'm sorry, Stacey. I have to go. I'm sorry to have disturbed you," I said with a lump in my throat, disconnecting the call.

She made me realize just how naive I was that I didn't know Ben at all. I hurried to gather my things to leave. I was so upset and busy stuffing things into my purse that I ran into someone while leaving my table.

"Tamara?"

"Marcus," I whispered.

"Hey, are you okay? I saw you when I walked in. You looked upset," he said.

"I'm sorry," I said, trying to gather my composure. "I'll be fine."

"No, have a seat. I can't allow you to drive like this. You are literally shaking."

"Thank you."

Not a word was exchanged between us as we sat there sipping our coffees in silence. He always had a calming effect on me. I don't know if it was his presence or what, but it needed to be bottled and sold. I guess that's what makes him a great doctor.

"Are you ready to talk about it?" He asked, drawing me out of my thoughts.

"No. I shouldn't burden you with my problems."

"Why not? I think it was meant for me to find you here at my favorite table, of all places."

"Your favorite table?"

"Whenever I do get a chance to come in, I try to grab this

table.”

“Wow. This is where I also try to sit whenever I come in.”

“There you have it. Today, you and I were destined to meet. Now tell me, what has you so distraught?”

I poured my soul out until it was empty to him, including my not-so-proud moments with Phillip. I figured I’d get some type of response from him regarding it, but he showed no reaction at all.

“So, do you believe Stacey was telling you the truth about your husband?”

“I don’t know. What she described is what is happening to me now. Something or someone has him distracted.”

“What are you planning to do about it?”

“I plan to keep my eyes open.”

“And if you find out that he is moving on with someone else?”

“It’s over for me. I learned a painful lesson by not taking

the time to ask questions, listen, understand, and wait. That lesson cost me you.”

“I hated that for the both of us, but in time, all things were revealed. My heart hasn’t changed towards you, Tamara. I have been keeping myself busy with work, so that I wouldn’t think of you as much. Believe it or not, I actually met someone the same day you and I parted ways, but I knew dating anyone at that moment would only cause more hurt, so I pretty much spent my time here and at the hospital.”

“I regret the day I chose my career over my heart. I did not know that things would have changed career-wise for me. I would’ve been next in line for a promotion had I stayed at Yeldon. Granted, the money wouldn’t have been the same, but I would have earned it on my own, rather than being placed in a position.”

“Don’t sell yourself short. I believe you do make a difference at H & G. That investment firm is top-notch. Even if you were “placed,” as you say, I think your being there was a good move. Look at you now, stomping with the bigwigs and calling the shots.”

“Thanks, but it doesn’t feel that way.”

“One thing I have learned is that living in the past is a prison all to itself. It is better to learn from the past, live in the present, and prepare for the future as best you can.”

“You’re right, Marcus, but I have to see this to the end, come what may.”

“And I believe that you will. You owe yourself that much.”

Chapter 20

BENJAMIN

Kherington is going to be the death of me. I thought, hoping to beat Tamara home. But as my luck would have it, she was pulling into the garage right behind me.

"Well, hello, stranger." I greeted her.

"Hey," she said, walking up to hug me.

"Where are you coming from?"

"The coffee shop, and you?" She asked, looking strange.

"Oh, you know me, Horizons."

"Mmm. Did you have a good time?"

"Of course, don't I always?" I laughed.

"I guess." She answered as we walked inside.

"Babe, is there something wrong? You don't seem like your normal self?"

"I'm fine."

"No, you're not. You're hiding something from me.

What's going on in that pretty head of yours?"

"Truthfully, I don't know where to begin, but for starters, why do you smell like perfume?"

"Huh, I smell like perfume," I said, sniffing my shirt, knowing damn well it came from Kherington. "I don't know. Maybe it's from you, babe." I said, trying to hug her.

"As expensive as it smells, it does not belong to me." She said, walking away.

"Babe, really? Uh, you know what, I'm such an idiot. Babe, I know where this is coming from. A patron at Horizons bumped into me when I was leaving."

"She must have held you close when she did."

"No. It was nothing like that. I know that there are trust issues plaguing us. But you must know how much I love you and wouldn't allow anything to come between us. You are my life." I said, looking her in the eyes.

"Your life, huh?" She asked, dismissing what I said.

"So you don't believe me?"

"What's there to believe? People bump into people every day. Goodnight, Ben." she said, walking away.

"Really, Tamara?" I yelled up the stairs.

I have to find a way to turn all of this around, and fast.

Chapter 21

KHERINGTON

My resentment wouldn't allow me to hold on to what I knew about Phillip. He had wronged me, and hopefully, I can stop him from doing the same to anyone else. The butthole should be home by now.

"What do I owe the pleasure of this phone call?" He asked sarcastically.

"I received confirmation of your package being delivered."

"Ah, yes. I have it here. It was safely placed at my front door. But surely you didn't call to tell me that I had a package?"

"I did, as a matter of fact. Plus, I wanted to discuss the contents inside of the box."

"Well, it can't be that much of a discussion. The package is quite small."

"That would be true of your package, but let's talk about

the box that you're holding."

"Hmph." He said. Okay, Kherington, let's play this mindless game. So far, I see a toothbrush that you could have discarded, an envelope, and what do we have here? You shouldn't have. A pint of my favorite whiskey and a glass. What are we celebrating?"

"The beginning of the end," I told him.

"I'll definitely drink to that." He said.

"But before you do, the envelope is the most important thing. Why don't you take a look inside?"

"Unless it is compensation for all the many years of mental anguish, pain, and suffering caused by you, I'm not interested in that envelope."

"So, you are stating that you are the only one who suffered through this entire ordeal?"

"I'm not saying that at all. You may have suffered, but it was because of your own doing."

"Really? Well, how is Ben's wife going to suffer?"

“What do you mean? What does Tamara have to do with any of this?” He asked angrily.

“Well, she is the most important thing to you, is she not? Are you going to do her the same way you did me? But wait, of course not; unlike me, you’re in love with her.”

“You have truly lost your mind. That is Ben’s wife that you are talking about.”

“Yes, I know. And you have yet to deny your feelings for her.”

“I don’t have to prove anything to anyone, especially not you. It was nice of you to send me the pint, but this is a little weird even for you, Kherington.”

“I see. So, you want to pretend as if I’m delusional? Okay. Open the envelope and see just how delusional I really am.”

<Silence>

“Hello.”

<Silence>

"Hello. I take it that your silence means you are finally seeing that I'm not as delusional as you once thought?"

"You can't be serious?"

"But I am."

"You had me followed?"

"Absolutely."

"Is this redemption or revenge for you?"

"It's hard to say."

"Why is that?"

"Well, when I couldn't get any straight answers from you for years, I did the next best thing. I hired someone who could give me the truth, and what I decide to do with that truth is up to me."

"You did all of this for what, Kherington? There was nothing left between us, and you knew that. This doesn't make any sense and it won't change anything."

"Maybe it will, maybe it won't, but something will change."

"Meaning?"

"I wonder how Ben will feel to learn his business partner has betrayed him by sleeping with his wife?"

"Like I said, nothing will change. So, if you thought having me followed would affect my money, business, or life, you are sadly mistaken."

"Last question. How does it feel to be in love with someone that you can't have?"

"What makes you think that I'm in love with anyone? Your problem is that you'll never know how it feels to be loved by me."

"I have moved on from you. I have someone who truly desires me."

"If that's the case, why are you so infatuated with me? Whatever man you do have won't be around for long. Please do him a solid by not guilt tripping him into staying with you, too."

"He won't have to worry about any of that."

"If I could have only been so lucky. Goodbye, Kherington." He said, hanging up.

Chapter 22

BENJAMIN

I was down three meetings and one to go before I could call it quits for the day and week. But it was always this busy at the end of a quarter. As usual, our three-ring circus was in full swing. Tamara and I held things down here while Phillip handled business coast to coast. I felt sorry for my boy. By the time he settled down on the east coast, he was back in the air and traveling to the west. All that traveling was grueling on the body. I offered to split some of the traveling responsibilities, but he declined. Before I got married, it was nothing for us to tag team our travels. He thought it would be better for me to stay, seeing how rocky things were already between Tamara and me. I agreed with him being a newlywed and all.

However, I wished I knew how a newlywed felt. Where was all of this wedded bliss everyone talked about? Since being married, it has been one thing after another. But it's my fault. I can admit it. Tamara is giving me the silent treatment after smelling perfume on my shirt. Nothing so far that I've tried to do has worked. I was at my wit's end. Unless she breaks the ice, I don't know what to do. And Kherington wasn't helping matters, either. She was on me heavy. I told her that we would have to chill for a while, but that pretty much sent her into overdrive. The only way I could get her to chill was by agreeing to meet her for lunch tomorrow. This way, I could be totally honest about where I'm going without having to make up some excuse.

Now, what can I do about Tamara? I sent her a text asking her to come into my office. Whether she does it or not will be a surprise to me. Since she didn't respond, I called her office.

"H & G Investments, Tamara speaking. How may I assist you?" She answered.

"Really?"

"Excuse me?"

"Did you see my text?" I asked her.

"Mr. Harris, I received your message but must decline your invitation at this time. I'm sure you understand?"

"We'll see about that," I said, hanging up to go to her office. "Tamara, I don't know where you get-" I immediately stopped talking when I saw that she had a full-blown meeting in progress. "Tamara, Jacob, Mitch, Randy, Sarah, Allison, guys. I am so sorry for barging in on your meeting. Please continue," I said, walking out and closing the door behind me.

***

I had just wrapped up my last meeting and went back to my office. I figured Tamara was already gone. Her door was closed, and the lights were off. To my surprise, she was waiting for me in my office.

"I thought you had left," I said.

"Oh no, not before seeing you eat crow." She said, laughing.

"I know I made a big fool out of myself, but you could have said you were in a meeting."

124

"I could have, but if you read your calendar, you too would have known. Is it always about what Ben wants?"

"Of course not. If that were the case, my wife wouldn't have given me the silent treatment for the past couple of days."

"Well, if my husband hadn't decided to come home smelling like another woman, maybe I wouldn't have."

"Tamara, alright, fine. I don't want to argue about this, especially since we are back speaking. Can we agree to disagree?"

"I guess." She said.

"What would my beautiful wife like to do this weekend?"

"I'm not sure. We could go out and have a nice dinner." She suggested.

"I like that. We hadn't had a date night in a while."

"No, we haven't. Where would you like to go? I heard about a few new restaurants I'd like to try. One is in the Summit and the other is in Uptown. We can also checkout the restaurants in Lakeview, too."

"Wherever you want to go, babe. Let me ask you something. Are you going to wear that dress I like?"

"Maybe." She said, smiling.

"What about those heels, too?" I asked her as we walked out of my office and closed the door behind us. I was getting excited just talking about it with her. I miss this. I missed us. Especially seeing her smile.

Walking to the car, I got a text message from Kherington. When I opened it, I almost dropped my phone. Thank God I was already sitting in the car when I did. Kherington had taken a picture of herself standing in the mirror nude with a caption saying we miss you. And I almost had a heart attack when Tamara knocked on the glass.

"What's wrong with you?" She asked.

"Nothing," I said, as I slid my phone down. "What's up?"

"Um, I wanted to know what time should we make our reservation? Let me show you what they have available at this new restaurant." She said, leaning in the window to scroll.

"Wait, go back up," I said. "What about this time?"

"Nine, that's a little late to eat, don't you think?"

"Not really. Besides, I was going to stop by one of my partna's and comeback in time to shower and dress. I was thinking we could make a night of it."

"And it's going to take you five hours to visit this person?"

"I'm not saying all that, but you know how things go."

"Un-huh, okay. I'll see you later."

"Tamara?" I called out to her as she walked away.

Chapter 23

TAMARA

I guess I had Boo Boo the Fool written across my forehead if he thought I was believing any of that mess. The same way he didn't want me to know that I saw him hide his phone was the same way I didn't want him to know that I placed an AirTag in his car. While he was looking at my phone, I slipped the tag in the back pouch of the driver's seat. No matter where he goes, I'll be able to find him. Benjamin Harris, you have finally run out of lies.

I went home to change into a sports bra, leggings, a hoodie, and a pair of Air Max. It was time to find out what was going on. According to this, he was only twenty minutes from the house. I typed the address of his location into Waze. His car had been there for an hour, the app said. Normally, I would have called Erica, but this was a solo trip. She would've talked me out of going, anyway. This was personal. I had to confirm with my eyes what my gut was already telling me.

Waze led me to a beautiful home community in the city of Hoover. One more left turn and my destination would be on the right. And there was his car. Whoever lived here had to park their car in the garage, because his car was the only car parked in the driveway. I sat there trying to think of the people he knew that I may have known that lived in Hoover, and I couldn't think of a single person.

What if this blows up in my face? I thought to myself. What kind of excuse could I give him if this turns out to be innocent? As nervous as I was, I had to know what was going on. I could no longer leave anything else up to chance. As soon as I got out of my car, my phone rang.

"Hello."

"Are you getting ready for our date tonight?"

"Ahh, yeah. You know me." I said, looking around frantically.

"I'll see you in a few. I'm out with the fellas."

"Oh, yeah."

"Yeah. I decided to come to Horizons for a few." He lied.

"Oh, that's cool," I said as I rang the doorbell.

"Hey, babe. Let me go. I'll see you soon." He said, hanging up.

You sure will, at Horizons, my ass.

Chapter 24

BENJAMIN

"Girl, how are you going to have me answer your door? I'm a guest in your home. Got me over here acting like a resident." I said, walking to the door.

"You have on more clothes than I do. Do you really want my neighbors to see me like this?" she asked, grabbing her robe.

"I have on one piece more than you, pants," I said as I went to answer the door. **"Oh, shit!"**

"Ben, what's wrong!?" Kherington asked, running to see what was going on.

"So this is who you're cheating with!?" Tamara asked, making her way inside.

"Tamara, what are you doing here? How did you know where I'd be?"

"I think the better question is, why are you here with her?"

"Babe, I can explain," I said, trying to keep Tamara separated from Kherington.

"So, you can explain why you are half dressed, and she is in a robe?"

"I was simply returning the favor. You slept with my man, so I slept with yours." Kherington said.

"Excuse me, bitch." Tamara asked, trying to get past me.

"**You heard me!** Try explaining what happened between you and Phillip."

"You mean the Phillip that tried desperately to get away from you for years, or the one who was elated when he did? Wait, maybe it was this Phillip, the one whose life you made a living hell because you are a conniving bitch. Have I confirmed the right Phillip yet? Because there's more."

"Tamara, that's enough. I think you should leave." I told her.

"No, Benjamin, being married to you was enough."

Tamara's words cut through me like a knife.

"What about you and Phillip?" Kherington asked.

"What about us? He is my friend, a genuine friend." She replied, rolling her eyes at me.

"No, I think it's a little more than that. Tell Ben about all the times you all spent together?" Kherington asked.

"She can't be serious, right?" I asked Tamara, hoping she would say or signal that it wasn't true. She gave me nothing. "I gotta go," I said.

"Why leave now, Ben? You lied to be here, remember?" she finally responded. "You thought I was stupid to believe all of those crazy lies. You may as well stay. You no longer have a reason to leave your partna." she told me.

"Tamara, I'm so sorry. Please forgive me." I said, reaching for her.

"No need for apologies, baby. Stay and enjoy yourself. It was worth it, right?"

"What makes you think it wasn't worth it?" Kherington asked.

"Un-huh, on that note, there's no need for me to take up

any more of your time. He's all yours, honey." Tamara said, getting ready to leave.

"So, it wasn't enough to have Ben's love, but you had to have Phillip's, too."

"Do you hear how you sound? Phillip, too? You helped to ruin a marriage, and all you can think about is who wants me? Are you crazy? The only someone who truly loves me in this scenario is me. I love myself enough to walk away from someone who isn't faithful. You should love yourself, too. Your self-esteem is so low that you allowed yourself to be with a man you had to guilt trip to keep. You are a successful, attractive woman who I once upon a time thought had right bright sense, but hey, what do I know? You could have had any man you wanted, but you chose him. Him, this one?" She said, pointing at me. "What's sadder to me is that you were so desperate that you went after someone who was married. I'm guessing the thought was if you couldn't have Phillip the way you wanted, you'd go after the next best thing, married or not. Good luck with this one, girl." Tamara said, laughing.

"Cute speech, but I don't need luck. You were with Phillip long before I slept with Ben. So, as far as I'm concerned, you jeopardized your marriage long before I ever could."

"You think so?"

"Oh, I know so. You just wait right here," Kherington said, leaving the room.

"So, is it true?" I asked her.

"Goodbye, Benjamin," Tamara said, leaving.

Chapter 25

KHERINGTON

"I'm so tired of people playing in my face and calling me a liar. I can prove every word that I said. Where did she go?" I asked a wounded Benjamin, who returned to the bedroom to get his clothes.

"She left."

"She left because I was not lying, and I would not lie to you, Ben. Here's everything you need. See the truth for yourself." I said, giving him the folder of everything I sent to Phillip.

"I can't believe this! How long have they been seeing each other?" He asked.

"I'm not sure, but the report is in chronological order. It'll show when it all began."

"Where were these pictures taken?"

"According to this report in Dallas."

"All that she had taken me through about Stacey, and this is what she does to me? I can't believe it. My wife and closest friend."

"Betrayal is heartbreaking, but revenge is so sweet."

"Revenge isn't always sweet, Kherington. I don't know if this was revenge for you, but it has wrecked my life literally. The woman that I love and the man I love like a brother, together, this hurts."

"I'm sorry, Ben. I wished there were more that I could do for you, but this is redemption for me."

"Thanks, Kherington, but I believe you have done enough." He said, walking to the front door.

"Are we still on for lunch tomorrow?" I asked, walking him out.

"No. I don't think it will be a good idea to continue seeing you," he said.

Chapter 26

BENJAMIN

I had a million thoughts swirling around in my head. I know I was probably pushing a hundred miles per hour on the freeway because I got home in no time. I held myself together the best way I could, but lost it once I saw that Tamara wasn't there.

"Where are you?" I asked, demanding an answer.

"My whereabouts are no longer your concern."

"Is it true?"

"Is what true?" She asked.

"Tamara, I swear to God if I find out you and Phillip have been sleeping with each other behind my back-"

"You'll what? What are you going to do? Phillip was my shoulder to cry on. He was the one there for me when you weren't. It was Phillip that dried my tears and talked me into not giving up on our marriage when I should've walked away. But my situation isn't your situation. All this time, I was blaming Stacey and myself for all of our problems, and as it turns out, it was you. And you know what? She was right about you."

"She was right about me?" Hearing Stacey's name was like pouring gasoline on a fire. It only made me angrier. "Stacey doesn't know a damn thing about me," I said, becoming more annoyed.

"You'd be wrong. I didn't see it until she showed me the real you, and once I saw it, I could not unsee it."

"I'm glad you and Stacey have rekindled your friendship, but when are you coming home so that we can talk about this?" I asked because I couldn't care less about Stacey.

"I'm not. There is nothing left to come back there for Benjamin. I'm filing for divorce first thing Monday morning."

"You're divorcing me when it was you and Phillip that betrayed me! And now you think you're about to take all my sh-"

<Call ended>

Chapter 27

TAMARA

Pick up Phillip, pick up!

"Hello."

"Thank goodness I reached you!" I sighed.

"Hey, you, what's going on?"

"Your girl."

"Kherington?'

"Yes!"

"What has she done now?"

"You mean other than sleeping with your business partner and my soon-to-be ex-husband?"

"They did what!?" He asked.

"Yeah, I caught him at her house. While there, she confronted me about you in front of him, and said she could prove it. I left before seeing anything. I came home to get a few of my things before he got there. Phillip, Ben hit the roof. That's why I am calling you right now. Please stay away from him. I've never seen him so irate."

"I'm not worried about me. My concern is for you. Are you going to be okay? Where are you going to stay?"

"A friend got me a hotel room for a couple of days until things blow over or until I decide where to go next. I didn't want to use any of my credit cards because he'd know where I was."

"That's smart. I'm just getting back in town and driving home. Kherington does have proof of us being together, but not us sleeping together."

"How?"

"She had me followed by a private investigator."

"But why?" I asked him.

"Trying to keep tabs on me."

"That's so crazy. I hate this for all of us."

"Yeah, me too. I guess it's my turn to be confronted. Ben is calling me now."

"Be careful."

"You, too."

PHILLIP

"Hello?"

"How could you do this to me? We're brothers, man."

"What did I do, Ben?"

"Man, you slept with my wife? My wife, man out of all people. How could you?"

"And you know this how?"

"Kherington showed me pictures and everything."

"So, there are pictures of Tamara and I in bed together?"

"No."

"So, how do you know that we slept together?"

"Well, the report talks about her going to your room and staying until the next day."

"And?"

"And you slept with my wife! My guy, I know how you operate. I know how you get down. It's me, remember?"

"Your knowing how I get down and proving I slept with Tamara are two different things."

"It's all semantics to me, bro."

"When Kherington gave me the same proof. I questioned it, but you believed it. We are different."

"She has no reason to lie to me."

"But she has every reason to lie on me. There's that difference again."

"You'll say anything to save your ass. But that slick talk won't work on me."

"But you'll take the word of a chick, right? I hear you've taken ownership of an old problem."

"Nah, I just slid through from time to time."

"There goes that difference again. I would never be so hasty, but you've allowed a temporary slide to ruin your marriage. What's crazier is, this was meant to be payback for me, but got you instead."

"Let's finish this discussion at Horizons," Ben suggested.

“I’m down.”

After hanging up with Ben, I called and spoke with Tamara for a while. She begged me not to go to Horizons, but I told her everything would be fine. We even talked about her coming over here if she wanted a change of scenery. No one would know that she was here, and she’d be safe. At least I’d feel better knowing she was close, just in case anything happened. I told her the code to open my garage from her phone. She had access to come and go as she pleased, and no one has ever had that. I could trust Tamara. I wished I could say the same of her husband. He often allowed things to cloud his better judgment, and sleeping with Kherington proved it.

Chapter 29

BENJAMIN

Phillip was taking his sweet time to come get this ass

whoopin. I hung up with him thirty minutes ago, and the longer

he makes me wait, the madder I get. I couldn't take the waiting

anymore and walked outside to get some air. Just as soon as I

stepped outside, here they come.

"Man, we've been calling you all night," TJ said.

"Why are y'all here? Let me guess, Tamara told Erica,

and she told you, and you called Ce."

"Ben, you have lost your damn mind, man. You want to

confront Phillip for the same thing you did to me. Make it make

sense. This isn't like you, bro," Ce said. "This is going too far,

and for what? You're about to jeopardize everything, Ben. I can't

believe you're out here doing what you said you'd never do,

fight a dude over a chic."

"Listen, I'm not trying to hear this shit. It's about the

principle, and that chic happens to be my wife.”

“Whatever happened to bros over hoes?” TJ asked.

“TJ, call my wife a hoe one more time. Y’all need to fall back and mind y’all own business. This is between Phillip and me. He betrayed me!”

“So, now you wanna get at me, because you’re about to mess up the church money. Think about how this will affect all of us, not just you.” He replied.

“All I know is you’re out here acting a damn fool over what, some hearsay?” Ce asked.

“This is not hearsay, bro. Y’all didn’t see what I saw or know what I know. He crossed the line.”

“And how exactly did I do that?” Phillip asked, walking up.

“It’s about time you showed your punk ass up. So, you sleep with my wife, and you don’t think I should have an issue with that?” I said, trying to get around TJ and Ce.

“Like I said over the phone, you don’t know if I did or

didn't."

"You're right. I can't prove that you didn't, but I'm about to whoop your ass because you did." I said, breaking through and connecting my fist to Phillip's face.

I must've blanked out because the next thing I knew, we were surrounded by phones flashing and people screaming. I was on the ground, pinned down by Ce and trying to catch my breath. As I looked around, I saw that TJ had Phillip pinned up against the wall.

"Ce, man, let me up."

"Not until you calm down. You know your stupid ass is about to go to jail, don't you?"

And as sure as he got the words out, here comes the cops.

"Everything is under control, officers. We have defused the situation." Ce said, helping me to my feet.

"That's good to know, but if you don't mind, we would like to assess the matter."

After the police spoke to us individually, we were told

that we needed to leave. At this point, I wished I could leave this entire day behind me.

After I picked up my phone and keys off the ground, it rang, and seeing who it was calling made me angry.

"Not now!" I yelled into the phone and hung up.

"That was her, wasn't it?" Phillip asked.

"Man, don't say nothing to me."

"Yeah, that was her." He said, wiping blood from the corner of his mouth.

"And if it was?" I answered, moving toward him.

"Hey, chill out," Ce said, who stepped in between us. "The police haven't left yet. If y'all start up with this bullshit again, you're both going to jail." He told us.

"I was just answering the man's question," I responded.

"Another difference. You're always quick to respond but slow to think."

"We can't be too different. It seems we have similar tastes in women."

"Do we?"

"Man, get out of here with that. It started when we were in college. You knew I liked Kherington, and you went after her."

"Did I go after her, or did she come after me? And yet you're sleeping with someone that I happily rid myself of."

"And then you decided it would be a good idea to move on with my wife."

"I haven't moved on with anyone. But the narrative paints a different picture. Tamara and I are only friends, nothing more. I was there for her during a difficult time."

"So was I for Kherington."

"Yeah, but Kherington's difficult time was made up in her head."

"What are you talking about? Kherington told me about the problems that you all were having."

"Like I said, that's the same thing that I was doing with Tamara, but the only difference is her issues were real. Kherington suffered a mental breakdown a few years ago and hasn't been right mentally since. The woman you knew years ago no longer exists. Think about how many times you've seen her throughout the years, Ben. As many gatherings and social events we've had, didn't you think it was strange that she wasn't there?"

"Damn, he's right, Ben. She wasn't," TJ said.

"She told me it was because you stopped inviting her to places."

"I pulled the plug on the entire thing when I found out she stopped taking her psych meds. I was tired of being blamed for her mental issues."

"Damn," Ce said.

"I believe that's when she set her plan in motion to get next to you. Do you think it was some coincidence that TJ found the two of you in the kitchen? No, I saw you first and sent him. She started kissing you right after seeing me. She tried to destroy what she thought would hurt me through you."

"He's telling the truth. He sent me in there to get you." TJ

150

said.

Well played, I thought. I felt like the biggest idiot on the planet.

"She didn't expect for Tamara to find out about the two of you. So, to keep you focused on her, she told you about the report-the same report that she thought she could blackmail me with, but in the end, she ended up ruining you, your partnership, friendship, and marriage. The difference between me and you, Ben, is that you fall victim to the women you entertain, and I don't." He said before leaving.

Chapter 30

TAMARA

I still can't believe Ben and Phillip got into a huge fight last night. After Erica told me about it, I immediately called Phillip to apologize. I felt so guilty. I'd like to think had I stayed home or stayed on the phone with Ben, none of this would have happened. I offered to take Phillip to the emergency room, but he declined. According to him, the only thing that hurt him at the moment was his pride. He told me that he had been using a pint of whiskey, which he had been gifted, as medicine. With things being as they are, I asked him what did this mean for H & G. There was no way they would continue as partners. He told me not to worry the firm would remain, but their friendship has ended. Phillip said that after cooler heads prevailed, he had a chance to fill Ben in on what he hadn't known about Kherington. There were still things she had said and done that he had not told anyone. I can't imagine. It is heartbreaking to know that he has kept this to himself for all these years.

Changing the subject, I asked him if it would be okay if I came by tomorrow, and he said it would. I thought it would be a friendly gesture to bring him some breakfast. It was the least that I could do, considering everything.

I've been trying to reach Phillip to tell him that I was on my way, and to ask him what he wanted for breakfast. I'm so glad that he gave me the code to the garage so I could let myself in. Where is this man? His car is here, but where is he?

"Phillip!?" I called out as I sat our breakfast down in the kitchen. "Phillip, boy, I've been calling you all morning long. Phillip? Where are you?" I asked.

"If these eggs get cold, don't blame me," I said, walking into the living room. **"Oh my God, Phillip!"**

Chapter 31

BENJAMIN

Man, who in the hell was this waking me out of my sleep by banging on my door? My head was killing me, and I was not in the mood.

"Benjamin Harris?"

"Yes." I said to the officer.

"I am Detective Rogers, and this is Officer Franklin. Would you mind if we came in and asked you a few questions?"

"No," I said, wondering what this was all about.

"Do you know a Phillip Gray?"

"Yes."

"What is your relationship to him, sir?"

"He is part co-owner of our investment firm and friend."

"When was the last time you saw or spoke with him, sir?"

"What is this about? Why are you all here?"

"Sir, when did you last see or speak to him?"

"It was last night."

"Did you see or speak to him in person?"

"I saw him." Now I was getting pissed. They were asking questions, but not answering any.

"And where did you all see each other?"

"We were at our night club Horizons."

"And why were you all there? Was it for business or something leisure?"

"We were there to talk."

"What did you all talk about?"

"I recently found out that he possibly slept with my wife, and I went to confront him.

"What time did this confrontation take place?"

"I'm not sure."

"Was Mr. Gray aware that you would be confronting him about these cheating allegations?"

"He was."

"Were there any other witnesses to this confrontation?"

"Yes."

"Did this confrontation turn violent?"

Why were they asking me questions that they already had answers to in a report? I guess Phillip was pressing charges.

"Yes, it ended up with us scuffling on the ground." I said annoyed.

"So, the two of you were in an altercation?"

"Yes."

"Was the police called?"

"Yes."

"Do you remember the officer's names that came out?"

"No. They spoke to both of us separately and advised us to go our separate ways."

"Who left first?"

"He did."

"Do you recall what time it was when he left?"

"No."

"What time did you leave?"

"I'm not sure. Maybe after midnight?"

"Where did you go after leaving Horizons?"

"I came home."

"And were you here all night?"

"Yes."

"Were you home alone?" The other officer asked.

"Yes."

"You mentioned your wife. Where was she?"

"I don't know. She and I argued yesterday and did not come home."

"What did you all argue about?"

"I would rather not say."

"You would rather not say?"

"Yes. It is personal. Are we done here?" I asked them.

"Unfortunately, no. We will need you to come with us for further questioning?"

"Further questioning about what?"

"I'm sorry to inform you of the passing of Phillip Gray."

"**His what!?** Phillip is dead? Oh my God." I asked, not sure if I was breathing myself.

***

Chapter 32

BENJAMIN

I was living a complete nightmare. It had been a week since Phillip's death, and the police were nowhere near close to having any answers. At the moment, his body was being prepared to be flown to a funeral home in Chicago. I planned on leaving out later this afternoon to help in any way I could. The news of his unexpected death sent shock waves throughout the company. We closed the firm in observance of Phillip. Any employee who wanted to be there at his service in Chicago was welcomed to attend.

Thinking back, I regret it all. I regret kissing Kherington, sleeping with her, and fighting with Phillip. He was my brother, my partner. Had I known, I would have never let my ego and emotions get the best of me, and because of it, my life was forever ruined.

My marriage was over, and there was no one to blame but

myself for it. I tried calling her, but my calls went straight to voicemail. I don't know where she is or anything. The only way I know that she's doing somewhat okay is through TJ. He told me that Tamara was the one who found Phillip. I wished I could comfort her, but I knew I was the last person she wanted to hear from. We were grieving over the same person, and there was nothing I could do to help her.

Guilt had driven me to the place of blaming myself for Phillip's death. When I went to the police station, Ce met me there. I was able to answer all of their questions. I thank God for my alarm system. He proved I was home all night and did not open any doors until the police came that morning. According to Ce, I was still not in the clear. If the autopsy came back that Phillip died from being in an altercation with me, I would be looking at some serious jail time.

That troubled me the most. To know that I caused someone that I cared about bodily harm did something to me. To make matters worse, there's no telling how long it will take for them to know what happened to Phillip. I had to do something sitting around the house was causing me to go stir-crazy. Just when I was about to hop into the shower, my phone rang.

"Hello."

"Mr. Harris?"

"Yes, this is he."

"This is Detective Bennett calling you from Birmingham PD. How are you doing today, sir?"

"I'm making it."

"I am one of the detectives working on Mr. Gray's case, and his toxicology report came back confirming high levels of arsenic poisoning in his body."

"Do you know of anyone that would want to harm your partner?"

"No, sir. I don't. I can't think of anyone. Phillip had a few friends, but he mainly kept to himself."

"Was he seeing anyone?"

"No. He and his girlfriend had broken up months ago."

"Would you happen to know her?"

"Yes, her name is Kherington Draker."

"According to my report, you all were friends, right?"

"Yes. We all went to college together."

"I see. Have you seen or heard from her?"

I thought about it. I hadn't talked to Kherington since the night I yelled at her. "No, sir. I haven't talked to her."

"We have been trying to reach her and were unable to make contact. It's to my understanding that she works at a local hospital here in the city."

"Yes, sir, she does."

"We have reached out to her last known employer. They informed us that she no longer works there, and hadn't been for months."

"I'm not sure when she changed jobs. She never once mentioned it." I told him.

"Well, should you hear from her, please pass on my contact information. It is imperative that we speak with her."

"I will pass along the message."

After hanging up with the detective, I called Kherington, only to be told by the recording that this was no longer a working number. What in the hell is going on?

Chapter 33

TAMARA

I don't know what I would've done if it weren't for

Marcus staying with me. Finding Phillip lying on the floor

helpless traumatized me. It's a wonder I had sense enough to call

the paramedics. Sadly, he was pronounced dead on the scene. I

answered all the police questions as best I could. I even told

them about the fight that had happened between him and Ben. At

the time, the police acted like it wasn't anything significant, but I

heard they later questioned Ben and let him go.

The good doctor has tried to get me to eat something, but

I couldn't. I didn't have an appetite. All I wanted to do was lie in

this bed. I've never had a friend to die before. Phillip and I had

an instant connection. We just got each other. It was something

special. I'll never forget the night we met, the slow dance in my

office, or his words of encouragement. I shared things with him I

didn't dare tell Ben. Phillip Gray was one hell of a man, and I will never forget him.

"It is good to see you smile," Marcus said, coming into his guest bedroom.

"Yeah, one day at a time."

"Does this mean you're going to eat something for me today?"

"Maybe," I said, following him into the kitchen.

"Good, because when I went into work, one of my co-workers gave me a bowl of homemade soup. I told her the other day that I was taking care of a sick friend, so she made it for you. She said she hoped that it would help."

"That was sweet of her. Who made it? Hold that thought. Ben is calling me for the hundredth time today."

"Answer the phone. If he's calling you like this, something's wrong." Marcus said.

"Hello!" I answered, annoyed.

"Tamara! Thank God you answered. Please don't hang up the phone. I need to talk to you. It's important."

"Ben, listen, if you are calling me to try to get me back,
save your breath because I don't-"

"**Tamara, listen!** It's not about that. **Your life is in
danger!**"

"My life is in danger?"

"Put the call on speakerphone," Marcus said.

"Yes, I just left the police station, and they have issued a
warrant out for Kherington's arrest."

"Kherington? Why?" I asked.

"They found evidence in her home that proves she may
have poisoned Phillip with arsenic and they recovered some
other information that suggested that you were next."

"**Me!**" This was too much. "Kherington doesn't have a
reason to come after me. Yes, we may have had words but that's
about it."

"She does if she's no longer taking her psychiatric meds
and feels that Phillip was in love with you. In her mind, you stole
him away from her. Kherington has gone off the deep end, and

unless they find her first, your life is in danger. According to the

police, she's been plotting this whole thing for months."

I was speechless.

"I'm sorry to butt into your conversation, but would this

Kherington have the last name of Drake, by any chance?"

Marcus asked.

"Yes," Ben answered. I could tell he wanted to know who

that was.

"Tamara, don't eat that soup!" Marcus yelled and

snatched the bowl away from me.

"I wasn't. I was just taking it out of the bag."

"Dr. Drake gave me this soup to give to you."

"Okay. Now, it's my turn to ask some questions," Ben

said. "Who are you, and how do you know Kherington?"

"I'm Tamara's friend Marcus, and I really don't know

her. She started working at my hospital about two months ago.

She came around the department and started talking to me and

the other staff. She was one of the doctors in pathology, so we didn't think much of it. We thought she was really nice."

"Mr. Elevator got it. Tamara, I don't know where you are, but this confirms that Kherington has been plotting against you, even going as far as to get next to your ex. You need to call the police immediately. I have the phone numbers of the detectives on Phillip's case. They need as much information as possible to capture her."

"Ben, can you-" was all I could say before this loud crashing sound interrupted me. "Hello Ben? Hello?"

"The call dropped." I told Marcus.

"What the hell?" He asked.

"I wished I knew. Let me see if I can call him back. Nope, it went straight to voicemail." I told him.

Chapter 34

STACEY

I'm so nervous. How do you tell a person who has chased you their entire life, telling them you didn't see them in that way, and after a Taco night, Don Julio, and a good time that they are the father of your child? I think what I fear the most is his response. I called him up and invited him to come over after he had gotten off from work.

Andrew was a good guy, and I can admit that. I have known him all my life, but he was like family to me. Our grandmothers were best friends, and they would try to put us together every chance they got. He and I attended the same high school. Back then, he wanted to pursue more, but it didn't last.

After graduating college, I knew I wanted a man who could give me more. I wanted the finer things in life and had met a man or two who could give me what I asked for. Andrew, on the other hand was nowhere near that financially. He did okay being a manager at the iron plant, but it wasn't enough for me.

I saved up enough money to keep me afloat for six months, but afterward, I was going to need help financially. After being fired from the bank, I purchased a Cobra plan so that we could have health coverage, and it was expensive. I also had a special insurance policy that if I lost my job that my house and car would be paid off, and they have been. I didn't have to worry about that, but everyday living, utilities, and food didn't come cheap. I was hoping to stay off from work until Cameron turned one, but that was contingent upon Ben being his father, and since I knew that he wasn't, it was time for me to revisit a few job leads.

My baby looked just like his dad. Jas and I found pictures from when we were babies and came across one of Andrew. They called him Red for a reason, and my baby was the same. His father had sandy-red hair and tiny brown freckles on his cheeks. I had a special name for him, Ginger Snap. He was very athletic and played many sports throughout school. Andrew was handsome and had girls at his beck and call, but it wasn't the same for me. After Big Mama begged and pleaded with me to go to the prom with Andrew, he asked, and I accepted. Later, I learned he had begged Ms. Earnestine, his grandmother, to ask Big Mama to help him. He told her if I accepted his invitation, he'd cut her grass for free the entire summer, and he did. We hung out every weekend until I left for college.

Looking back over our prom night, I had mixed emotions. My feelings inadvertently changed toward him after we won homecoming king and queen. I saw him in a different light after our first dance, which scared me. I didn't know what to feel or how to feel. And to this day, admittedly, those same feelings have helped me to keep him at arm's length. Especially after that night. My feelings concerning him had become extremely complicated.

I will never host another Taco night at my house ever again. Jasmine's man, Devontae, and Andrew are really good friends, so she thought it would be a good idea for the four of us to hang out at my house. We cooked the food, and the fellas brought the spirits. I don't know why I let Jasmine's heavy-handed self make the margaritas. She always doubled, if not tripled, the liquor in the drinks. The next thing I knew, we were all laughing and having a good time. No one was in any condition to drive. Thank God she lived next door. They left, and Andrew and I reminisced about old times. After one heartfelt confession and a passionate kiss, one thing led to another, and I woke up the next day in the arms of a man who would change my life forever.

The same man that had given me Cameron was now ringing my doorbell.

"Ginger Snap!" I said, giving him a huge hug.

"Hey, Stacey." He said, hugging me back.

"Come in and have a seat. Did you have a good day at work?'

"Thanks, yeah, I did. How about you?"

"It was good and busy. I'm sure Devontae has told you

that I had a baby?" I asked him as we sat down.

"Yeah, he did, and congratulations to you, by the way. I didn't want to cause any confusion between you and your man, so I fell back."

"Yeah, about that, um, who I thought was the father wasn't, and um. How do I say this? Um, I believe that you are."

"Say what?"

"Yeah, I think showing you would explain it better." I got up to go get Cameron so that he could see his son for himself. "Andrew, meet your son Cameron," I told him as we sat beside him.

"Oh my God, Stacey. He looks just like me. May I hold him?"

"Sure." I gently placed Cameron in his arms. I couldn't help but think this was how our father felt seeing and holding us for the first time. I melted.

"He is so perfect."

"Yeah, my little guy is."

"Our little guy." He corrected me.

Cameron squirmed and cooed until he found the perfect spot and slept in his daddy's arms. I had Andrew follow me to my bedroom to place him in his bassinet. I pulled the door up behind us, and we returned to the living room.

"Why didn't you tell me you were pregnant?" He asked.

"To be honest, I really didn't think the baby was yours."

"Now what?"

"That's why you are here. I wanted to tell you about him because I need your help or will need your help later. I got let go from the bank about three months ago. I had enough money at the time to carry us for six months, but it looks like I'll have to go back to work sooner than thought. What I need is financial support for Cameron. We can take a paternity test at this lab that keeps calling me or one of your choice."

"I have no problem with any of that. But I wish you would have told me. Do you know how hurt I felt to learn about your pregnancy through Devontae? I thought we were better than that. I know you said you weren't sure, but it feels like I was dismissed long before I ever became a candidate. You know, whatever I have, he has, but where does that leave us? I was already upset with you on how you ghosted my ass."

"I know. I wasn't in the right head space to entertain what you were offering."

"And now?"

"I'm still not sure."

"You know how important family is to me, Stacey."

"Yes, I do." I sighed. "But I'm not sure if what you're offering is enough. I'm just being honest. I don't want to hurt you."

"What is it that you are needing from me?"

"Financial stability."

"I have that."

"Yes, but it's limited stability."

"And where's your stability? You are asking about things that you yourself don't have."

"But with the right man, I won't need to."

"So, what I'm hearing from you is that you want to be a

kept woman. You want someone to take care of you. You don't need a man to genuinely love, protect, and provide for you."

"I didn't say that."

"It doesn't sound like you want a man at all, but a sugar daddy. Set the appointment up, and I'll be in touch with you about when and where we will be taking the paternity test." He said, before leaving.

Chapter 35

BENJAMIN

Before calling Tamara back, I had to get out and see how much damage was done to my car.

"Hey, sorry about that," I said when she answered the phone.

"I was wondering what had happened to you."

"I hit a big pothole and damaged the passenger tire and bumper. I hope I hadn't cracked my rim."

"I didn't know what happened. All this talk about Kherington has me in shock."

"I can't believe it myself, but it is real. According to the police, she murdered Phillip using poison. What you told me will help them in their investigation and possibly locate her. I was trying to find Detective Bennett's phone number to give to you when I hit the hole, but I'm home now and can give you everything you need." I provided Tamara with the detective's phone number.

"Tamara, I know you might not like this, but I think it may be a good idea for you to have a security detail until they find her. The police didn't go into details about all they had, but I think it would be a good idea to have around."

"I don't know about this, Ben. This is too much."

"I know, but from what I was told, she has some type of vendetta against you. She was successful once, and giving Marcus that soup means she has gotten closer."

"You're right."

"No one knows if or when she will strike again, but I'm going to try my best to keep everyone safe. I've even added double security for our buildings, even Horizons."

"How would this work?"

"Basically, wherever you go, there will be someone with you."

"I don't know what to do. Should I leave, stay, or what? Where can I go?"

"Well, if you are at Marcus's house, you're not safe there either. If she knows who he is, she also knows where he lives. Think about it and let me know. I hired security for my parents and TJ's homes. They are not at risk, but I didn't want to take any chances with their lives either."

Chapter 36

TAMARA

I accepted Ben's offer of security after talking to Marcus about it. I really didn't know which way to turn. All I knew was that I wanted to be safe, and there was no way that I could go back home. I felt safe and comfortable at Marcus's. Erica also offered me a place to stay, but with the baby being on the way and the possibility of Ben stopping by, I declined her invitation.

There was nothing going on between Marcus and me. Just having him near was enough. I was mentally, emotionally, and physically exhausted. I needed someone to be there for me through all of this, and he has been without question.

After hanging up with Ben, I called the detective and set up a time to meet with him and his team the next day. Upon our coming to the police station, I was introduced to my security detail. They were the biggest, meanest-looking men I'd ever seen in my life. And just as Ben said, wherever I went, they went.

They were waiting outside of the interrogation room until our interview was finished.

"Thank you, Mrs. Harris for coming down and speaking to us. Mr. Harris informed us that you had some additional information to give us regarding the case."

"Yes, I have my friend Dr. Marcus Worthington here with me, and he can give you more information about Kherington. She gave him some soup yesterday to give to me. After hearing from Ben that she was a suspect in Phillip's death, we felt that something may have been wrong with the soup."

"It is possible. By chance, did you all bring it with you?"

"We did. I place it in a plastic storage bag." Marcus said.

"Dr. Worthington, how do you know the alleged suspect?"

"She started working at Mercy Hospital-"

"I'm sorry to cut you off, but did you say Mercy Hospital?"

"Yes, sir. She's been working there for a few months."

"Alright, please continue," the detective said, taking notes.

"One night, a team of surgeons and I were in the O.R. working a five-car accident. We had just finished with the last trauma case when she came up to ask us about a specimen. We were clueless as to what she was talking about, and that's when she apologized for being on the wrong floor. She introduced herself as Dr. Kherington Drake of Pathology. The next day, she saw a few of us having lunch and asked if she could join us. She didn't say much, but from time to time, she would join us. I was getting off from work the other day and said I had to go and see about a sick friend. She asked me if I was coming to work the next day, and I told her I was. That's when she gave me the soup to give to Tamara, saying she hoped it would help her feel better."

"This is good. Did you ever mention who your sick friend was by name? Have you been back to work since receiving the soup?"

"No, not at all. I'm off until next week."

"What do you think, Johnathan?" The detective asked the other. "Do you think we can flush her out through the doctor?"

"It's possible. She'll have to think that Mrs. Harris is dead or extremely sick." The other detective responded.

"Wait, what?" I asked.

"These are just ideas that we are kicking around. We know this would be a lot to add to an already full plate." He said to me. "Let's do this. Let's send the soup down to the lab, test it, and see what they come back with. From there, we can come up with a plan." He said to the officer who had taken the soup. "While we wait for those results, let me explain what we have so far. When we obtained a search warrant to search the alleged assailant's home. We found some pretty damning information. When we arrived, no one was present except her housekeeper. According to her, Ms. Draker had not been there in quite some time. We conducted our search and found a board, documents, pictures, and the same poison that killed Mr. Gray. According to our findings, she created some kind of board that was hidden under her bed. Pictures of you, Dr. Worthington, Mr. Harris, the deceased, and another woman were on this board. She had Mr. Gray's picture crossed out and your picture circled along with a line drawn to Dr. Worthington. There were some other things, like baby things, listed as if she was completing a list of sorts. Do you know if she was pregnant, trying to become pregnant, or planning to adopt?"

"Not to my knowledge, but I didn't know her like that, to even be privileged to that information."

"But why am I a part of this? The only one I know in this scenario is Tamara?" Marcus asked.

"To answer your question, Dr. Worthington, you are the connection she used to get to Mrs. Harris. Somehow, she found out that the two of you knew each other."

"How?" He asked.

"She had us investigated and followed," I answered.

"She did, and that is why we have him in the other interrogation room. Hopefully, he can help shed some light on the things pictured that don't quite fit. I have to ask you more questions. Did you and the deceased have a romantic relationship?"

"No, we didn't. Phillip and I were good friends. He was there for me when I needed someone to lean on."

"Hmm, somehow she thinks that you may have taken him away from her."

"That's not true. He had broken things off with her months ago. He told to me that there were things that had happened between them that he had never told anyone but was glad to be out of it."

"That sounds similar to what Mr. Harris told us about them. Once again, not to pry, but I'm having to ask. Were you aware of the romantic involvement between Mr. Harris and Ms. Draker?"

"Yes, I followed my husband to Kherington's house and confronted them together."

"We have a positive match for arsenic." The officer said,

coming into the room.

"I was afraid of that. Now, we will add attempted murder to her list of charges."

"Oh, my God!" I said in disbelief.

"Mrs. Harris, we appreciate you and Dr. Worthington for coming in to talk to us. We are doing all we can to find her. She has evaded us twice. Until we can bring her in, please stay close to your security detail. It is you she has set her sights on, and unfortunately, we don't believe she's going to stop until she succeeds."

Chapter 37

ERICA

My heart and prayers went out to Phillip's family. I know the shocking news of his death rocked our world. You talk about somebody that you couldn't say a bad thing about, and that would be him. It's always those that are the closest to you that cause the most harm. Kherington must have snapped. I know I didn't know her that well, but murder. Something had to happen to cause her to do this.

I knew Tamara and Marcus had gone to the police station yesterday. I wanted to give her some time to process what was going on. I really wished she would have stayed here with us, but I understood why she didn't. I gave my friend a call to check on her.

"Hello."

"Hey, girl, what are you up to?"

"I'm over here packing clothes for the funeral

tomorrow.”

“I wish I could come.”

“Girl, TJ wish you would hop on a plane,” Tamara said,
laughing.

It felt good to hear her laugh. “Honey, don’t even talk
about it. I had to convince him to go to the funeral. My mother
will be here with me until the baby comes.”

“That’s good! Please give her a big hug for me. I can’t
wait to see her at the baby shower next week.”

“I know we both can’t wait to see you. I miss you,
friend.”

“I miss you too, but with everything going on, you know
I can’t risk placing you and the baby in harm’s way.”

“I know. It’s just not fair.” I told her.

“But it will be over soon. I pray it will anyway.”

“Has anyone seen or heard from her?”

“Not to my knowledge. Marcus went back to work early
for the police, only to find out she quit.”

“Girl, what?”

"Yes, ma'am. She quit the day she gave him that soup to give to me."

"Where could she have gone?"

"Who knows? I know it's not to her residence because they have that under surveillance."

"I just can't believe Kherington, out of all people, would do such a thing."

"She did. And if you had seen how she was acting when I confronted Ben at her house, you, too, would believe it."

"She had everyone fooled."

"Everyone but Phillip."

"I wished he could have told us about her."

"That wasn't his style. No matter how crazy it was, he took it to the grave."

"True. I feel helpless."

"Me and you both, Erica. Switching the subject, what is JJ up to?"

"Girl, he's probably driving his mother up the wall

talking about the baby.”

“He’s excited about becoming a big brother.”

“He certainly acts like it. I miss my little company keeper. Speaking of keeping company, how’s Marcus?”

“He’s good. I had a moment the other night, and he heard me crying and held me until I fell asleep. My life has never been this torn up before. But Marcus has been solid for me, and I appreciate it. He wanted to attend Phillip’s service with me, but I told him I would be fine with going alone. It’s not like I would be alone, anyway.”

“You sure won’t with how this security detail is set up. I’d be careful to sneeze around them.”

“When I tell you they don’t play. Marcus brought me my favorite coffee and muffin from the coffee shop. Do you know they tested it before I could have it?”

“Un-huh, that’s why they had to know what our menu was and where it was coming from ahead of time .”

“I’ll be so glad when this is over with. This can’t be life.”

Tamara said.

"It's what it is for the time being. Let us just be glad that we are safe."

"You're right, Erica. I just want my life back. I feel like I'm under house arrest."

"I have a little more freedom than you do, but not by much."

"Let me finish packing, and I'll call you before I board. I love you, girlie."

"To the moon and back, bestie," I told her before hanging up.

Chapter 38

BENJAMIN

This is one of the hardest days of my life. Pain and heartbreak had surrounded us as we prepared to say goodbye to Phillip. It was all I could do not to break down at Mother Gray's feet. I was distraught. I fought with my brother over what I had come to realize was nothing. Whatever they did or did not do was between the two of them. I had my own burdens to bear, and the sorrow I felt was ripping my heart apart. I was on the program to speak next, and I didn't see how it was going to be possible.

"Now, we will hear from Benjamin Harris."

"Thank you." I sighed. "I wish I could express how much I am going to miss him," I said, gripping the podium. "Um, we-" was all I could get out before breaking down and having to be sat down.

"Phillip was one of a kind, and we will truly miss him. I

personally got a chance to meet Phillip when he made me an offer I simply could not refuse. If you knew Phillip, you know." They laughed. "Phillip was charming and had a way with words. He was also dedicated to helping others so on behalf of the H & G family, we are equally committed to keeping his memory alive by opening the Phillip Gray Foundation for Mental Health and Wellness. May his loving spirit and kindness be embedded into the hearts and minds of everyone this foundation helps." Tamara said before taking her seat.

After the service, I found Tamara, who had just finished speaking to someone.

"Thank you for what you did up there. You were amazing."

"It's the least I can do for all he has done for me. I think he would be pleased." She said, smiling.

"I think so, too. Do you think we-"

"Hey, baby," Pop said, interrupting me. They came over to hug Tamara.

"Hey, family. How are you all?"

"No, baby, how are you doing?" Mama asked.

"One day at a time, one day at a time."

"Are you and Ben coming over to Eugenia's house for dinner? I know she'll be glad to have you."

"No ma'am. I will be flying out tonight."

"Hmm, oh, okay," Pop said, looking at me.

"Well, you two, stay safe and be careful."

"Only Tamara is leaving. I'm not leaving until tomorrow. So, I will be joining you at Mother Gray's house."

"So you're staying, and she's leaving?" Pop asked.

"It was good seeing both of you. I'm going to go speak with a few more people from H & G before heading back to the hotel." She said, hugging them.

"I don't know what you've done, but whatever it is, fix it." Pop whispered in my ear.

If only he knew how much I wished I could.

Chapter 39

TAMARA

I thought I was ready to return to work, and I was okay until I walked past Phillip's office. Seeing it open, dark, and empty disturbed me. It reminded me of finality. Knowing I'd never see him sitting behind that desk, hearing his voice, or having another conversation about his cars broke my heart. I rushed into my office and slammed the door behind me. It was not fair. This place has now become too much to bear, partly because of Phillip and the other just walked through my door.

"Good morning. I heard you come in. Are you okay? " Ben asked.

"No."

"I knew today was going to be hard for all of us. I had our meetings canceled for the rest of the week. We have many things to discuss regarding the business and foundation.

"Yeah, sure," I said.

"What would you like to discuss first, business or our personal life?"

"Let's discuss the business first." I said.

"Well, I was thinking about keeping the firm's name the same, but I do not plan on replacing Phillip. I will take over both roles and hire other staff to assist."

"What about my role?"

"What about your role?" He asked.

"You will need to hire or promote someone to cover this position as well."

"Are you quitting?"

"In a sense, but more like swapping roles. I want to head up the foundation."

"Wow. Do you think you're ready for that?"

"I am."

"You want to be away from me that bad that you'll switch companies?"

"Ben, what did you think was going to happen? You

thought I was going to be with you after knowing what you did?"

"You can't blame a man for trying. I just was hoping that you would at least go to marriage counseling or something with me."

"Where was the marriage counseling when you were sleeping with the enemy?"

"The same place it was when Phillip slept with you."

"Really?"

"Yes. Phillip never denied you two sleeping together. That's why we fought. One thing he wasn't, Tamara, was a liar. But that's not why we're here."

"Okay, why are we here, then?"

"Because I need my wife."

"You need what?" He had jokes this morning. "Ben, are you serious?"

"Yes. We still love each other, and it will take counseling to help us get back to the place we once were."

"Why would I even consider that? When you slept with

both Stacey and Kherington. You did this before and during our marriage. Your love for me must be bipolar, baby."

"Seriously? My love for you is steadfast."

"I guess your love was steadfast for Stacey, too, when you made a down payment on her house."

"Say what? I know you tripping now because I've never spent that kind of bread on no woman other than you."

"That's what she told me, and that you wanted to buy her a car."

"Can I sit here?" He asked, sitting at my desk, to log into my computer. "Do you remember when she bought the townhouse?"

"Yes."

"Bet. Here are all of my banking and business accounts. Put in the year she purchased the townhouse and see if there's a lump sum of money missing from these accounts?"

I did as he asked. "I don't see anything from that time period."

"Exactly. I don't know why you would listen to her,
anyway. She lies to hurt people, Tamara. Don't you know that?"

"She also told me about the day you all slept together.
Say what you will. She may have lied about the money, but she
has you pegged in behavior patterns. She told me how you would
act when you have lost interest or are bored with what you have.
Just as she said you'd act, you did, and she called it. Like I said,
bipolar love."

"A hit dog will holler. That much I know to be true."

"And that means."

"Everything she may have accused me of, the same
applies to her. She'll say anything to turn you against me."

"She didn't say anything that I had not experienced. Your
actions speak volumes."

"Here's our reality. We are both guilty of doing the same
things. It's just I was caught, and you weren't."

"You're missing the point. I could never trust you again.
Why be married to someone you can't trust?"

"That is the point. I'm willing to forgive and trust you. I know I have made some terrible mistakes, and Phillip helped me to see that. That night before he left, he said to me that I was fast to react and slow to think. Things would've been much different had I considered how my life would be affected. I would've definitely made better choices."

"Phillip thought the world of you. He had to be sick of me talking about you. I remember going back and forth about leaving you, and I guess he had heard enough that day," I said, laughing at the memory. "Because he told me being very snippy to fight for my marriage if I thought it was worth saving." I said.

"We were lucky to have him."

"Yeah, we were. I don't know how your thinking first would have changed things for Phillip, though."

"I don't know, Tamara, it could have. Had I not driven you into his arms for comfort, maybe she wouldn't have killed him." He said.

"Kherington was a ticking time bomb that was ready to

blow.”

“I’m just hoping she’s caught soon, for all our sakes.”

“Has she been in contact with anyone?” I asked.

“The only people she knew within our circle were TJ and me, but she hasn’t reached out to us.”

“I know, I’d feel better knowing she was in custody.”

“How are things with your ex? I’m sure he’s happy to have you back?”

“There’s nothing going on between Marcus and I. He is a supportive friend, that’s it.”

“Well, I wished you could have stayed longer and explained things to Pop. I needed a supportive friend because he gave me the business after you left.”

“Good.”

“Good? Okay. That’s why he wants to see the both of us tomorrow evening in his office at the church. Come with your Bible,” he said, standing up to leave.

“Why do I have to come?” I said, following him. “I

didn't do anything wrong."

"Explain that to him. Love you, bye," he said, kissing me on the cheek.

Chapter 40

BENJAMIN

If Tamara thought I was going to face the music by myself, she had another thing coming. Pop was very upset when she left. For the most part, I had kept my parents in the dark about the circumstances surrounding Phillip's death. They weren't aware of all the intricate details, but I had a feeling the truth was going to come out tonight.

Talking to Tamara yesterday gave me a little hope of our marriage being salvaged. I know we had a long road ahead of us, but knowing that she had not moved on and was still wearing her ring gave me some promise. I was glad she believed me after proving Stacey had lied.

Tamara and I pulled up at the same time with security in tow. Until Kherington was caught, this was our new normal.

"Hey, Pop! We're here." I said, holding the door open for Tamara.

"Come on in and take a seat. How's my sweet girl doing?" He asked Tamara, giving her a hug. She got a hug, and I get the side-eye, okay? I already know how this evening is about to go.

"I'm doing well, Pop. Ben told me you wanted to see us about something."

"I know y'all are wondering why you're here, but I called you together for a purpose. Only to see your faces when I asked if y'all were serious. Is this really what the young folks are doing in twenty twenty-four? Businesses, partnerships, friendships, and a marriage just destroyed, and over what? Y'all had to know it was going to get back to me. Are y'all serious is the question? I wished I could sit here and be in shock and disbelief, but at the moment, I've heard and seen enough to know y'all can't be for real. Lord, give us strength because we need you today. Son? Really?"

"Well, Pop-"

"It's always well Pop with you, isn't it, Benjamin? I

raised you to be a man of integrity. Do you remember what you told me and your mother about this woman? Do you remember what you said? Because I certainly do. Tamara, you are the daughter I've always wanted, and it hurts me deeply to learn what may have transpired amongst the four of you. Phillip, God rest his soul, and Kherington were like family as well, so how on earth did we get here? Yes, I said we because we are a family, and families, especially mine, don't do stuff like this. Unless y'all agreed to switch partners and failed to tell the rest of us, but hey that's neither here nor there."

"Pop, I mean no disrespect, and I know this is not a laughing matter, but where did you get this information? Because none of it is true."

"Well, somebody sent me an email with this information and pictures."

"Kherington," Tamara and I said in unison. "Pop, I know this is confusing, but this goes deeper than what you know. Unfortunately, there are no simple answers. I have made some awful decisions, and talking about them would only make matters worse."

"I appreciate your honesty, son, but I've always told you to consider the cost of your actions. Was it worth it? Was she worth destroying your family over?"

"Pop, no, it wasn't. I put everything at risk. Now you are being drawn into something that you had nothing to do with."

"Pop, I can't speak for Ben, but I feel like all of this is my fault. Had I not leaned on Phillip so much, he'd probably be here today," she said, crying. All I could do was hold her.

We were all broken and there was nothing I could do to fix it. Pop handed Tamara some Kleenex and a bottle of water.

"Tamara, I'm so sorry that you feel the need to place this burden on your shoulders. But this was not your fault, baby. Kherington is not right in her mind. Evil did this baby, not you. Kherington needs medical help, and the longer she evades the authorities, the worse it will be for all of us. Let your heart not be troubled by evildoers, for in due time, they will reap what they sow."

"Thanks, Pop." She said, leaning against my chest.

"Pop, can you forward that email to me? Maybe the detective can use it to track her location."

"I hope so, because enough is enough of this madness. Your mother is already feeding the security guards."

"She's what?"

"Yep, every time I look up, she takes a sandwich or something out there to them."

"Lawd mama, you're not supposed to feed the men. I'll talk to her."

Tamara jumped when her phone buzzed.

"What's wrong?" I asked.

"The alarm at Phillip's house just went off."

"Call the police! That has to be Kherington."

Chapter 41

STACEY

After Andrew left, I felt a sense of loss. He and I had never mixed words. How did a beautiful moment change so swiftly? I told Jasmine everything that had happened when she came over. She mentioned something that I never really gave thought. She asked if I thought I had daddy issues, because I had all the classic symptoms. She said I kept Andrew at an arm's distance because I really liked him, and was afraid he would leave me.

After hearing that, I thought about how most of the men I dated didn't want anything from me but to be arm candy, and the only one that ever wanted my heart, I pushed away. It made me wonder if I thought I was incapable of being loved.

I called Andrew and asked him if we could talk and ride together to the lab. He agreed to come by early, but I could tell that he was still salty with me.

"Hey." He said, dryly after I opened the door.

"Hey."

"What's up? What did you want to talk to me about?" He said, as we sat down.

"I wanted to apologize for our conversation the other day. I was wrong to question whether you were financially stable, and for not telling you about the pregnancy."

"Stacey, I am hurt. I don't think you understand how much. The thought of being disregarded because I didn't make seven figures angered me."

"I'm sorry, Andrew. You're the most solid guy I ever had in my life. And I don't know what you see or want from me. I knew my role in what those other men wanted, but you were different. I guess what I'm fearing the most is your leaving me."

"Stacey, I'm here for you, and I want you to know that it's not just for your body. I know this is scary. I've seen you around a few times with different guys, and I didn't say anything, because in my heart, I knew it wouldn't last. I knew they didn't see what I saw in you therefore, they couldn't give you what I could, actual love. You've entrusted your heart to all the wrong ones in the name of stability. All I'm asking is for the opportunity to provide for you and Cameron the right way. I've loved you girl ever since we were children, and I know you, flaws and all. Give your heart to me, the only one who can promise to keep it and never break it. I want a life with you. I am offering you stability and love. Let me love you the way you need to be. I am committed to you. I've laid it all out. You know how I feel about you. You've always known. The ball is in your court."

"I really want to, but how?"

"By trusting me."

"This is so surreal for me. When you said what you said to me the other day and left, I'm not going to lie, I felt a real loss, like my world had come to an end."

"I owe you an apology. I shouldn't have spoken to you that way. I was upset and frustrated. Imagine wanting something your whole life, getting close enough to have it as your own, only for someone to snatch it away because they thought you weren't worthy of having it."

"I get it. I mean, I understand where you are coming from. The night Cameron was conceived, you expressed your feelings for me, and I regret not trusting what I felt was real in heart."

"And now?"

"I want this. I want you. I want us." I answered.

After kissing me, he said, "I'm entrusting my heart to you. Please don't break it. Come on, let's get our little man ready to go. It's almost a waste of time and money to even do this."

"Yeah, but I need it done for another reason."

"What do you mean?" He asked, handing me a pamper to change Cameron.

"Well, as I told you before, I didn't know who Cameron's father was, so I told two different men about my pregnancy. One man had a paternity test done while we were in the hospital, and he was excluded. Two weeks ago, the second man reached out to me about taking the test. I informed him that he was not

Cameron's father. I didn't need a test to tell me what I could see

every time I saw my baby's face."

"Yeah, he is the spitting image of me."

"He wasn't trying to hear any of it. He said he needed to

be sure."

"Now, don't get angry with me when I say this, but he's

right."

"What?"

"Just hear me out. Believe it or not, Stacey, so many men

have gotten caught up over the word of a woman. That man

thinks he's off the hook, and the next thing he knows, he's being

hauled off to court and being made to pay back child support for

someone he was told wasn't his."

"Hmph, I know about mine."

"Now you do, but that wasn't always the case. Since we

are in the process of having the test done today, see if he can

meet us at the lab. If he is as persistent as you say, he won't miss the opportunity to close this chapter.”

Just as Andrew said, Ben agreed to meet us there. I felt like I was dreaming, but this was the real thing. I was falling in love with Andrew, and I could finally give myself permission to do it.

We loaded Cameron into the backseat of Andrew’s black-on-black GMC Denali truck and headed to the lab. Okay, pockets, I was impressed. I guess he was right. I didn’t know about his financial stability, and I thank him for having patience with me because this could have gone bad.

“What will our grandmothers think about us getting together?” I asked, holding his hand while he drove.

“Knowing mine, she’d say about damn time.”

We laughed because, knowing her, that’s exactly what she’d say.

“Watch this.” I called Big Mama.

“Hello.”

“What are you doing?”

“Over here talking to Stine.”

"Really? Put me on speakerphone."

"Okay. What's up?"

"Guess what?"

"What?" they said.

"Andrew is Cameron's father, and we're together."

"Girl, I thought you called to tell us something, hell we knew that."

"Ma'am?" I asked as Andrew laughed.

"Yeah, honey, Stine and I were on Facetime when she saw Cameron and said look at baby Drew, and I looked at him and said sho is. They thank they slick."

"We were waiting for y'all to come out with it." Ms. Earnestine said.

"Are y'all bringing our baby over here?" Big Mama asked.

"Yes, ma'am, right after we run this errand."

"Alright, keep him covered. I don't want him to catch no

chill.”

“Yes, ma’am. We’ll see you all soon. Bye.”

“What are we going to do with them?”

“Give them five more to keep them busy.” He said.

“Listen, I just got through with that one. I’m going to need a little more time.”

Laughing, he said, “And guess how much time I’m going to give you, a few minutes. We have to make up for lost time.”

“Keep it up, and I’m going to tell Ms. Earnestine on you.” I said, laughing.

After parking the truck, he opened my door, and grabbed Cameron. We registered our information and waited for Ben to arrive.

The nurse came up to us and introduced herself. She said she was the one that I spoke with over the phone, and would be taking Cameron to the back to be swabbed. I stood up to go with them, but she said that wouldn’t be necessary, that she would bring him right back. Some time had passed, and I wondered when she was going to return with Cameron.

"Andrew Lassiter?" The woman called.

"Hey, a nurse took my son to the back, and she has not returned with him. Is everything okay?"

"I'm sorry, sir. What are you having done today?" She asked, confused.

"A paternity test. My girlfriend made the appointment the other day." He said, pointing at me. "And the nurse took our son to the back to be tested."

"You said a nurse took your son to the back?"

"Yes, she had on blue scrubs like yours and went through that door. Baby, what did she say her name was?" he asked me.

"She said her name was Nurse Draker. I also spoke with her to make this appointment." I said, standing up because something wasn't right.

Frantically she says, "sir, I apologize, but we don't have a nurse by that name on our staff, and the door you pointing to leads to an alley behind this building. Excuse me, **Allison, call**

the police. Someone has just abducted a baby!" She yelled

as she rushed to open the back door in hopes of stopping the

abduction.

A Thin Line Between

Happily & Ever After

Coming in 2025

Your review matters!

Please enter your review of this book online at Amazon.

I'll love to hear from you:

Please email me at ddmiles.relationshipreflections@gmail.com,

Want to read more? See the link below:

Website at https://relationshipreflections.org.